When life goes

OFF TRACK

Liezl Shnookal

First edition published in Australia in 2014 by
Bush Telegraph XPress
P.O. Box 76, St Andrews, VIC Australia 3761
http://www.bushtelegraphxpress.com

Edition: 2

Publisher: Inspiring Publishers,
P.O. Box 159, Calwell, ACT Australia 2905
Email: publishaspg@gmail.com
http://www.inspiringpublishers.com

A catalogue record for this book is available from the National Library of Australia

National Library of Australia The Prepublication Data Service

Author: Liezl Shnookal
Title: Off Track
Genre: Modern Contemporary Fiction

Paperback ISBN: 978-1-922920-99-7
ePub2 ISBN: 978-1-923087-99-6
PDF eBook ISBN: 978-1-923087-98-9

CONTENTS

Chapter One...1

Chapter Two...3

Chapter Three..7

Chapter Four 11

Chapter Five..15

Chapter Six..18

Chapter Seven...23

Chapter Eight..27

Chapter Nine 31

Chapter Ten...33

Chapter Eleven 36

Chapter Twelve 42

Chapter Thirteen 47

Chapter Fourteen 53

Chapter Fifteen..58

Chapter Sixteen 66

Chapter Seventeen 71

Chapter Eighteen..74

Chapter Nineteen 80

Chapter Twenty 87

Chapter Twenty-One 92

Chapter Twenty-Two...96

Chapter Twenty-Three..100

Chapter Twenty-Four 106

Chapter Twenty-Five 110

Chapter Twenty-Six 115

Chapter Twenty-Seven 120

Chapter Twenty-Eight 126

Chapter Twenty-Nine 130

Chapter Thirty 133

Chapter Thirty-One 134

Chapter Thirty-Two 138

In loving memory of Murray Norman

ONE

This story isn't about me. After all, there really isn't much to say about someone like me. Lucy Runelli: short, skinny, dark-brown hair, grey eyes. The only person who reckons I'm pretty is my father. I'm not especially good at anything, except maybe reading – big deal. I'm half-Italian, half-Australian.

Luckily this book is about someone else.

I met Scott Allen in 1969. I was fourteen and as usual, I was spending the summer holidays at our beach house in Shoreham. My sixteen-year-old sister Gina and I were cantering our horses along the shoreline early one evening when a boy in tattered jeans sauntered across our path.

'Shit! Watch where you're going!' he yelled as we just managed to avoid him.

Gina reined in her horse and shouted over her shoulder, 'You're the idiot who walked in front of us!'

Suddenly she swivelled around in her saddle. 'Hey, aren't you Rob's brother?'

'Yeah, so what's it to you?'

It turned out that Gina had met Rob at a party in Melbourne a few weeks earlier. Scott had been there too. The way in which my sister leapt off her horse to talk to him was a sure sign that the brother was someone special. I hoped for Gina's sake that Rob was better looking than Scott.

The two of them chatted for a while. I watched the boy take a cigarette from a crumpled Marlboro packet and light up, even though he was clearly far too young to be smoking. My sister made some ridiculous joke about his name, pretending to be confused about whether it was Scott Allen or Alan Scott. Ha! I was certain that she'd remembered Rob's surname perfectly. Nevertheless, I was impressed by the way she kept the conversation going.

To my surprise, Scott strolled over to where I was still sitting on my horse and looked up at me. His cigarette finished, he ground the butt into the sand with a dirty bare foot and then, very slowly and suggestively, he winked at me.

'What's your problem?' I asked, scowling down at him.

But he just winked again.

'Gina, we have to go. It's getting dark.' Without waiting for a reply, I set off at a fast trot across the beach towards home.

I didn't think much of Scott Allen, that first time I met him. Sure, his blue eyes sort of twinkled when he grinned, but basically he seemed to be a dirty, rough, rude lout.

Three days later, when I saw him again, my opinion didn't change.

TWO

It was Christmas Eve and we always celebrated that special night in a spirit of family togetherness.

'Get lost, Lucy! I'm wrapping up your present,' Gina screamed as I tried to enter our shared bedroom.

So I wandered back into the living room and for want of anything better to do, rearranged the tinsel and baubles on the Christmas pine tree. My father was in his customary chair, writing out cheques for each of us. He called it 'doing his Christmas shopping'. Why he never took the trouble to buy us presents, I don't know. It was a hot night and even though the open windows had screens on them, my father was occasionally slapping his ankles. Mosquitoes loved his Italian blood.

My twelve-year-old brother came into the room and asked crossly, 'Who's pinched the scissors and sticky tape?'

'Gina is using them. You'll just have to wait,' I replied.

'Damn!'

'Andy, I've told you before not to swear!' my father said, then, 'Kate! Turn that bloody record off!' as my mother turned up the volume on her favourite Christmas record.

'Why? There's nothing like the *Hallelujah Chorus* to brighten up a house at this time of year.'

Our dog began to bark and we only just managed to hear a knock on the door above the general din. The visitor was a tall dark boy of about seventeen, who was introduced by Gina as Rob Allen. Relieved, I moved a stack of presents off the couch to make room for him. Rob was handsome, after all.

'Nice place you have here, Dr Runelli,' he said.

'Yes, I built this little shack myself a long time ago,' my father replied. 'And do you spend your holidays here, or are you a local?'

'Holidays only, unfortunately.' The boy managed a quick glance at Gina, who flicked back her long hair and smiled. I never knew my sister could look so pretty.

'And what does your father do for a living?' My mother could always be counted on to ask our friends that question.

'Actually, it's my stepfather. He's a judge,' Rob answered and settled more comfortably into his chair. 'My mother owns Baxters Booksellers.' Suddenly there was a loud crash outside, followed by a string of four-letter words. Rob groaned.

The door was pushed open and there in the doorway was Scott, grinning stupidly at us all. The smell of alcohol filled the room. To my horror he staggered towards the couch and flopped down beside me.

'How'd ya be?' he slurred into my face.

I raised my hands to block his kiss.

'Shit! Can't a man be friendly on Chrissie Eve?'

'A friend of yours, dear?' my mother asked, frowning.

'Who the hell is this?' my father demanded, also glaring at me as if somehow I were to blame.

Scott slumped against the back of his seat and gazed around the room.

'How should I know—?' I began.

'I'm terribly sorry, Dr Runelli, this is Scott, my younger brother. He had a bit too much to drink at dinner,' Rob explained smoothly. 'He must have followed me here.'

'Oh, I see,' my father muttered. 'And are there any more like him at home?'

'Oh no,' he laughed. 'I have an older brother called Duncan who is doing Law at Melbourne Uni. He hopes to go to Oxford eventually. Then there's Fiona, who's only eight, but is already doing advanced maths.' Scott fell off the couch and began to wrestle with our dog Buster on the floor. We all ignored them.

'Where do you go to school?' my mother continued the investigation.

Rob mentioned the name of a prestigious private boys school in Melbourne. There was a contemptuous snort from Scott as he picked himself up and fell into a chair.

'You'll appreciate our school when you grow up a bit,' said Rob.

My brother was looking at Scott with interest. 'How old are you?' he asked.

'Fifteen, going on twenty-five.'

Scott lit a cigarette and inhaled deeply. At the appearance of a Marlboro packet, my father beamed and sidled over. He was always giving up smoking.

'Smoke, mate?' the boy asked.

'Always good for a cough,' my father the doctor replied as he took one.

They sat there, sharing an ashtray and smiling at each other through the haze.

'So what team do you barrack for, Scott?'

'The Pies, of course! Who else?'

With Dad and Scott now happily engrossed in an argument about football and the interrogation apparently over, Gina and Rob moved to a corner of the room to talk privately. Andy and

I began to play cards while my mother went into the kitchen to do the dishes.

Andy had just beaten me for the second game in a row when I saw Rob pulling his brother to his feet.

'It's time to go home to bed. Come on,' he said.

Swaying as he stood, Scott grumbled, 'But I don't wanna go yet. The Doc and I were just starting on politics.'

However, he was pushed through the door and into the darkness outside. Rob said goodnight and shook my father's hand. He looked at Gina, smiled, and was gone.

A neighbour's dog began to bark and we could hear Scott's voice, still complaining, fading into the distance.

THREE

Boxing Day. I sat up to examine the state of my tan. After two hours' sunbaking, it was looking quite good. I adjusted my brand-new pink bikini and checked out what else was happening on the beach.

Nothing, as usual. The tide was coming in. Andy was reading a comic book and Gina seemed asleep. My father, of course, wasn't there – he hated the beach – but my mother sat in her chair, a newspaper spread out over her knees. Down at the water's edge, some toddlers were trying to drown themselves. Heat haze shimmered above the sand and a catamaran skimmed across the sea. Somewhere a transistor was on, but not loud enough for me to hear the songs.

I sighed. I'd been coming to that beach all my life and frankly sometimes I wish I hadn't. It was always the same. Boring. The only excitement we ever had was when some day-tripper got his car bogged in the sand launching his boat. Or when Buster decided to lift his leg against someone's beach umbrella.

Still, a beach is a beach, I thought and lay back on my towel. I rolled onto my stomach, hitched up my bikini bottom and nestled my chin into a hollow in the sand.

I was almost asleep when I felt the vibration of approaching footsteps.

'G'day!' It was Scott's voice.

'Hi!' Gina answered. 'Where's the rest of your family? I thought you'd all be down here.' I knew she'd be hopefully scanning the beach for Rob.

'Nah,' Scott scoffed, 'they're all too damn lazy to walk down the track.'

There was a disappointed sigh and a pause in the conversation. I had just begun to raise my head from the towel when a huge dump of sand landed on my back.

'Hey!' Scott said. 'Aren't ya talking to me today?'

I leapt up, furious.

'How dare you, you—' I stopped, distracted. 'Scott, what on earth are you wearing?'

'Like it? I got it for Christmas. I don't think I'll ever take it off.' He turned around slowly, like he was some kind of a model, showing off his new sheepskin jacket.

I couldn't help myself, I just had to laugh. He stood there in the blistering heat, wearing shorts and a thick woolly coat.

'Well, yeah, I know it's hot but that's why I cut off the sleeves. Anyway, wanna swim?'

'But how can you go for a swim when you just said that you'll never take off your precious jacket?' I asked, somewhat smugly.

'For you, sweetie,' he replied, 'I'd get completely naked!'

I heard my mother groan as she turned over the pages of her newspaper.

Scott proceeded to rip off his coat, then grinned and picked me up.

'Hey!' I screamed. 'Put me down!'

He carried me into the sea, even though I was kicking and struggling with all my strength. Finally, when I felt the cold water around my waist, I bit him as hard as I could. He dropped me immediately.

'Bitch!' he shouted.

I fell into the water. When I surfaced again, he was waiting for me.

'You weren't really scared, were you?' His blue eyes studied my face. 'Sorry, maybe I was a bit rough.'

Before I could think of a reply, he swam off. I adjusted my bathers and tried to make a dignified retreat back to my towel. I thought I'd succeeded, until I saw the smirk on Andy's face. Sometimes I'd like to kill that little brat.

When Scott returned from his swim he didn't even glance in my direction. He flopped down next to Andy and together they began talking about different types of cars.

After a while Gina sat up and began madly brushing her hair. Following her gaze I saw Rob walking up the beach with two other people. She waved at them and they came over. Fiona Allen was just a kid. The oldest of the family, Duncan, immediately fanned out his towel, sat down on it, adjusted his glasses and began to read a book. He obviously was not going to be a whole lot of fun.

Andy suggested a game of cricket. As everyone completely ignored my pained expression and began arguing about teams, I decided to head home rather than be forced to join in. I picked up my things, walked along the shoreline and made my way up the track through the pine forest. Since it was a steep climb, I paused for a few minutes at the top to catch my breath. Looking back down over the beach, I could just make out my mother, standing ankle deep in the water, talking to someone. Her huge ridiculous hat always made her easy to spot.

The cricket match was in full swing. I watched Rob whack the ball hard, sending it into the sea. My sister Gina was jumping up and down enthusiastically. Scott raced off in hot pursuit of the ball and leapt into the water. Andy was flapping his arms, obviously encouraging him, while little Fiona was simply standing around looking useless. There was no sign of Duncan.

I'd barely turned away from the scene when I heard a loud shriek. Fiona was standing stock still, her hands over her mouth, and I saw Scott plunge underwater, half a second before a catamaran zoomed straight over the place where he'd just been.

I held my breath. An eternity passed. Nothing. I felt sick.

But suddenly a head bobbed up and there was Scott. He flung an arm into the air and cheerfully waved to the others. He'd got the ball. Fiona looked as if she might be crying.

I guess the whole thing made me wonder about Scott. I mean, what sort of person risks his life just to get a ball? Surely he must have seen the yacht so close in to shore and known the danger he was in? He really was a crazy kid.

My pounding heart began to settle. After all, it was really nothing to do with me. I shrugged my shoulders and continued to walk along the well-trodden track.

FOUR

New Year's Eve. The start of a whole new decade! It's funny, but New Year's Eve had never seemed such a big deal before. Now that I was fourteen, it loomed as a major event. I decided against wearing a dress and put on my best jeans and a new red shirt, then made the mistake of looking in the mirror. I was such a skinny, runty kind of kid. When would I ever start to grow?

We were having a party at our place. Lots of families were coming over for a barbecue and hopefully other people would turn up afterwards. I walked into the kitchen to find my mother rushing around frantically.

'Where have you been? Take this out to the table,' she cried, thrusting a large plate of buttered bread into my hands. 'And grab the tomato sauce! Watch out that Buster doesn't eat the bread!'

That's my mother for you, always in a fuss about something. I wish I could describe her to you, but I can't. Maybe it's because I see her every day, or maybe it's because she just looks like a mother – anybody's mother.

Anyway, loaded up with food, I walked outside to find my father and Andy in front of the barbecue, fiercely arguing about the best way to keep the small flame alight.

Naturally they were so busy with their fight that the fire went out.

'How's the barbecue going, Leo?' my mother called.

'Huh! Ask your son!' my father shouted and stormed off.

Andy watched him go, then threw down a piece of wood and marched off in the direction of the beach.

'What's happening?' Gina demanded, appearing from the bungalow.

'Dad and Andy are at it again. They were meant to light the fire,' I explained, rolling my eyes. 'Hey, you look terrific!'

She really did, too. She had on a blue mini dress and was even wearing make-up.

Gina and I lit the barbecue and eventually people arrived. Buster did manage to steal a whole plateful of uncooked meat and Andy didn't come home for hours, but apart from that, the meal went well.

At about nine o'clock, the Allen kids showed up.

'G'day. Any tucker left? Rin Tin Tin is hungry.' Scott grinned.

Beside him was a huge, beautiful German Shepherd, who took one look at Buster and began growling. Rob immediately intervened, grabbing his dog's collar and marching off homeward with Rin Tin Tin.

All kinds of people were crowded around the barbecue, caught in the glare of the outside lights. My parents were drinking heavily, particularly my father. Italian music was blaring out of the old reel-to-reel tape machine that was set up on the table, and some people had begun to dance. My father leapt to his feet, shouting, 'I've forgotten my dancing hat.'

'No, Leo. No!' my mother cried, but he was already running into the house.

He reappeared within seconds, putting on his Scottish beret as he ran.

'Aha! Now I'm Angus McLeo!' he laughed as he attempted the Highland fling.

My father was born in Italy but had come to Australia when he was six. When he'd been drinking, his concept of his national identity became confused. Scottish, Australian, Italian – it really didn't matter. For me, he was simply a dag.

Just then Scott leapt into the light and threw himself in front of my father, joining him in the dance. Arms and legs flying, the pair whirled around the fire. Everyone clapped, shouting encouragement, but no one else dared to get to their feet. When the song finished, Scott yelled, 'Hey, you haven't seen anything yet, Doc. I'll go home and get *my* hat!'

Ten minutes later he returned, panting, wearing a white Arab headdress, held in place by a piece of coloured rope. My father greeted this strangely dressed boy as if he were a long-lost relative.

'Scott, my boy, you deserve another beer. Here's to us!' he said as the two of them downed their cans.

I headed into the house. A Beatles record was blaring and I could see that Gina and Rob were part of the large crowd dancing inside. Andy was sitting at the table, playing cards with two cousins. I talked to them for a while but a quarter of an hour with my brother is usually the most I could stand, so I soon wandered away in search of better entertainment.

But when I opened the door to the sunroom, I discovered Scott Allen, astride one of the saddles that we kept in there. I shouted at him, but it only made him jog up and down even more, on my best saddle! Andy came running when he heard me yell, then stood there like an idiot laughing at Scott, Arabian headdress brushed back, pretending he was riding a horse.

'Stop! You'll wreck it! Don't you know it ruins a saddle to sit on it when it's not properly supported?' I snapped.

He completely ignored me as he continued to ride through his imaginary desert. Suddenly someone turned up the volume on the stereo and the song 'Revolution' came blasting through the open door. Thankfully Scott leapt out of the saddle, threw off his costume hat and danced into the next room, waving a clenched fist in the air.

Gina met him with an answering raised fist and together they danced wildly into the crowd. I checked that my saddle hadn't been damaged before I too joined the dancing mob.

At five to twelve I went to the toilet and stayed there until ten past twelve, when I knew that I would be safe from all the kissing. Welcome to the 1970s, I thought, as I left the protection of the toilet to re-enter the party. 'Here Comes the Sun' was playing and everyone was dancing so wildly that the record kept skipping, making it difficult to stay with the beat. I danced for a while but there were too many slow tracks on *Abbey Road* and so eventually I decided to call it a night and headed for the bungalow that I shared with Gina.

I changed into my pyjamas, grabbed some paper and a biro and got into bed. I wrote at the top of the page 'My New Year's Resolutions – 1970' and then thought for a while. Finally I wrote my list: '1. Buy a miniskirt and some boots. 2. Get my hair cut into a bob. 3. Be kinder to Andy. 4. Learn tennis. 5. Get all A's for English.' That'll do, I decided. Outside people were still talking and laughing around the barbecue, and I heard Dad invite Scott to go with him to another party. I switched off the light and in spite of the din, drifted off to sleep.

FIVE

I awoke the next morning to the sound of rain hammering on our corrugated-iron roof. Maybe 1970 isn't going to be such a great year after all, I thought, and went back to sleep. When I opened my eyes it was ten-thirty. Still raining. Going into the kitchen I found an absolute disaster zone, with dishes and leftover food everywhere. My parents were obviously still nursing heavy hangovers in bed. As there's never much to do when it isn't beach weather, I took my breakfast back to bed and began to read *Jane Eyre.* I was just at the part where Jane was locked in the red-room when Gina woke up, grabbed some clothes and disappeared. I continued reading for the rest of the day, undisturbed.

By evening the sky had cleared. I got up again to discover the big clean-up was underway and so I quickly escaped, unnoticed, out the front gate. I ambled down the track and onto the beach. Removing my thongs, I felt the sand damp and cold between my toes.

I wandered along the shoreline, enjoying the peace and tranquillity until I heard a shout. Turning around I saw Scott racing towards me, his sheepskin jacket flying out behind him.

'Oh hello, Scott.'

Suddenly I was rugby-tackled to the ground.

'Do you always have to attack first and talk second?' I grumbled as I picked myself up off the sand. He just grinned.

'So how's your head? Bad headache?' I asked hopefully.

'Nup, I felt a bit crook this morning but now I feel fine. Great party last night!'

'Yes, it was.' I didn't know what else to say.

Scott made me feel very uneasy, although he didn't seem to notice. He slouched along beside me, hands in his jeans pockets, as we walked up the beach.

'I really wish my stepfather was more like your old man,' he sighed.

'In what way?'

'He's a big-time judge at some city court and so he acts like God at our place. Everything the old bastard says to me begins with, "Now Scott, my boy, don't . . ." or "Goodness, not at the dinner table . . ."' Scott wagged his index finger at me.

We both laughed.

'Anyway, he's boring. Hey, I've got a car, did you know? An old Holden, a beaut little paddock-thrasher. We're on twenty acres at home in Eltham, which means I've got plenty of room to drive around. My mates help me 'cos the car's a bit stuffed. Omo hangs onto the door to stop it from opening and Spike changes the gears – it takes two hands. Another mate has to sit out on the back, holding the exhaust pipe on with wire. We always go for a burn when someone has enough money to buy petrol.'

He looked at me to see if I was impressed. I frowned to show that I wasn't, but he continued anyway, telling me the details of one particular time when they smashed into a tree. Suddenly he looked down at me and said, 'You're bloody short, aren't you?'

I stopped walking and glared at him. He had hit on a sore point.

'So? I can't help that, can I?' I shouted.

'Hey, wait a minute. I wasn't criticising. I think you're kind of cute that way.'

But he had chosen exactly the wrong word.

'Cute?' I sneered. 'When you're short, you're never beautiful or graceful or sophisticated. No, you're always just cute! Everyone pats you on the head when you're small. "Oh, isn't she cute!" people say, patting away. What am I meant to do – wag my tail? "And how old are you, dear? . . . Well, well, are you really fourteen? You're so little, you certainly don't look your age!" It's not my fault that I look young, and they should know enough to shut up. They can all go to hell and so can you, Scott Allen!'

I picked up some rocks and flung them furiously into the sea one after the other.

Gradually I began to calm down. I turned around to find that Scott was still there, drawing patterns in the sand with a bare foot and looking at me strangely. He bent down quickly, grabbed a rock and handed it to me.

'Thanks,' I said and threw it as far as I could.

'My name's Scotchie.'

We both threw rocks at the sea for a while.

'Let's keep walking,' he suggested.

The colours of the sunset shifted and changed while we walked along the beach in silence. The waves rolled in and the seagulls bobbed up and down behind them. Eventually night began to fall, so we headed back up the track. We reached my driveway and when I turned towards the house, his tall shape continued to move along the road.

'Scotchie?' I called through the darkness.

'Yeah?'

'See you later.'

SIX

The Allen boys began to be regular visitors, dropping in every day. I never saw much of Rob because he'd disappear somewhere with Gina, almost as soon as he'd arrived. Those two were really becoming impossible.

Anyway, there were other kids who used our place as their home away from home. Richard and John were two boys who frequently hung around, reading our large selection of comics. Richard was a particular friend of Andy's, having spent a previous summer bombing bull ants with him. John was a huge hulk of a kid, his one claim to fame being his feet, which overhung a foolscap sheet of paper. Even at sixteen, he had to get his shoes specially made.

John and Richard were brothers, although they didn't like to admit it very often. Once, during an exceptionally bad argument, John had kicked Richard as hard as he could in the backside. John, as a result, had broken one of his immense toes while Richard was completely unharmed. This had taught John 'a big lesson in life', as he put it, that violence simply doesn't pay. Consequently he became a super-pacifist and each time Richard began to tell the broken toe story (as he frequently did), John would leave the room, his face red with shame.

John quickly became a good mate of Scotchie's and was immediately dubbed Little John. Scotchie complained often that it took forever to get anywhere if John was with him, but John would only shrug his broad shoulders in response. There was no way he was going to speed up for anybody. So it was decided that John would be given a head start on trips and this new arrangement seemed to work well for all concerned.

Scotchie regularly dragged John over to our house to visit my father, and on one particular afternoon, Scotchie arrived to find my father outside near the barbecue.

'G'day, Doc! What's up?'

'I'm just burning off some rubbish in the incinerator.'

They both loaded in more paper and together watched as the flames flared higher.

'I think that a ginger beer would go down well, don't you?' my father suggested. He made his own ginger beer in the shed, resulting in occasional explosions, and it was considered to be very drinkable.

'Beauty. Hey, Little John, it's about time! You almost missed out on sampling the latest batch of the Doc's brew,' Scotchie called as John finally arrived.

'Andy, bring us out some glasses and a bottle, there's a good lad,' my father said.

My brother, the idiot, was always quick to obey. In fact, I don't think he minded playing the role of domestic slave so long as it was Scotchie he was serving. But if I'd been Andy, I would have resented the way Dad seemed to enjoy another kid's company more than his own son's. Andy was never invited to sit down and join in the conversation.

So John, Scotchie and my father took their customary seats around the unlit barbecue. Unnoticed in the adjoining paddock, I eavesdropped on their conversation as I brushed my horse.

'Terrible news in the paper again this morning about South Africa,' my father began. 'Did you see?'

Scotchie nodded. 'More blacks arrested. Apartheid is such bullshit. We shouldn't be going over there to play cricket.'

'But it's sport. Nothing to do with politics,' argued my father, a huge fan of test matches. 'Besides, it's not our business what's happening in another country.'

Scotchie snorted. 'Only whites can vote and play in major teams – that's wrong! We shouldn't be supporting this kind of injustice in any way!'

'I'm not sure that a boycott is the solution.'

'At least the Irish are trying to do something, protesting against the Springbok rugby team!'

'Now, there's another huge problem – the fight between the Catholics and the Protestants in Ireland,' Dad sighed.

'Bloody religion. God has a lot to answer for!'

'I don't think that you can blame God for The Troubles in Ireland.'

'But isn't he meant to look after us all?' Scotchie asked angrily. 'How can there be a God when there are so many people fighting against one another and in his name? And what about all those people starving to death all over the world?'

John said nothing as he wriggled uncomfortably in his chair. I happened to know that he was quite religious but he certainly wasn't about to argue against his friend Scotchie. Besides, he rarely joined in the conversation at the best of times, preferring to sit and listen.

There was only one thing that my father enjoyed as much as a debate, and that was fixing things. Mending broken junk was his other favourite hobby.

'Can you just give me a hand here for ten minutes?' my father would ask.

Well, we all knew that our father's idea of 'ten minutes' usually meant two hours and so we learnt to disappear from view very quickly. But Scotchie never seemed to mind 'giving a hand'.

One day when the pair was in the garage sorting through heaps of useless rubbish, Scotchie found the old wheelchair. It had been taken from the surgery years before, but no one had got around to making it mobile again. Scotchie instantly set about restoring it, with lots of help from my father. Scotchie hardly came out of the garage for three whole days and I even heard him talking to the chair a few times. Soon we were taking turns to wheel each other everywhere. Unfortunately it didn't work very well on sand, so we had to keep to the roads.

'Who's coming for a spin around the block?' Scotchie asked one afternoon, not long after we had all come back from the beach.

I shook my head and continued my card game with John and Richard. As usual, Rob and Gina were not to be found, so Andy and Scotchie were the only ones who went off together.

An hour later my mother answered a knock on the door. There stood two policemen and behind them, the boys. Andy looked slightly pale while Scotchie, head down, kept picking the wool out of his sheepskin jacket.

'Are these kids yours?' one policeman asked. Without waiting for a reply, he went on, 'Next time, lady, do us a favour and keep them at home. These little delinquents shouldn't be allowed out on the streets.' With a parting scowl at the boys, the policemen left.

Apparently Andy had wheeled Scotchie down a steep hill. When the chair had begun to pick up speed, my brother had let go and Scotchie had zoomed down the main road. Passing the general store he'd noticed a police car and given them a two-fingered salute, while shouting 'Piss off pigs'. Unfortunately the policemen had taken offence and sped after him in their car, siren blaring and lights flashing. When they'd caught up with the runaway wheelchair they'd waited until Andy came panting up, even though Scotchie was madly trying to wave him away.

'The bastards!' pronounced Scotchie. 'They screwed up the best ride of the whole summer! Those coppers talked about an "unlicensed vehicle" and "speeding in a built-up area" – what a load of crap! They almost gave me a ticket!'

John and I were both laughing as we followed Scotchie out through the door, but to our surprise, Scotchie was extremely angry. He picked up an axe that was resting against the wall of the house and walked over to the wheelchair that he had so painstakingly restored. He lunged at it with the axe, making a huge gash in the seat padding.

'What the hell are you doing that for?' John yelled and grabbed the axe in the middle of the next swing.

'Why aren't I ever allowed to have fun?' Scotchie raged, beside himself with fury. 'It's not fair!'

He tried to get the axe back but John's huge hands held it in a vice-like grip. Deathly quiet, Scotchie watched as the axe was returned to its place.

'You're all deadshits!' he screamed and gave the wheelchair a vicious kick before he stormed out the front gate.

'So what's up with him?' I asked, bewildered.

'Scotchie is going to end up in disaster one of these days if he doesn't learn to control himself,' John muttered darkly.

'Maybe.'

At any rate, one thing I knew for certain was that my parents weren't going to let us take the wheelchair out again. Not after all the trouble it had caused.

SEVEN

Naturally I was right. So with our only form of transport gone (except for the horses) we went back to walking. Strolls along the beach became our nightly ritual, begun by Gina and Rob, and taken up by the rest of us. John, Richard and Scotchie seemed to share a common stock of dirty songs and would sing them at the tops of their voices on the way. Since no one ever remembered to bring a torch, somebody usually tripped over a tree root on our journey down the track in the dark.

One particular night it was my brother who was stupid enough to fall over, although of course Andy claimed that he was pushed. When they reached the sand, he and Scotchie had a skipping race, which ended in a long shouted list of swear words as Scotchie stubbed his foot against a rock. The moon came out from behind a cloud and I watched Gina and Rob quickly disappear up the beach together. John lay down on his back to examine the stars.

I ran to join my sister but quickly realised my mistake, for just as I reached them, they sprang apart and Gina snapped, 'What on earth do you want?'

'Oh, I was just wondering if you were going riding tomorrow morning,' I stammered.

'Lucy, buzz off!'

Hurt, I watched them walk off, hand in hand. Scotchie came rushing up.

'Are you blind? Can't you see that they want to be left alone?'

'But they're . . . too young for that sort of thing.'

'They're teenagers and plenty old enough! Besides, I'll have you know that I had my first real girlfriend years ago,' Scotchie boasted.

'What do you mean?' My attention was no longer on my sister.

'Don't you understand anything? I'm a man of experience.'

Fortunately Andy and Richard came running up just at that moment and I was very glad that the topic of conversation suddenly changed.

'So there you are!' Andy said. 'Scotchie, let's go back to your place. It's too cold on the beach tonight.'

'My place? No way! It's much better at your joint, believe me!'

Scotchie had never taken us back to his house. Not even once. But this time we all insisted, and although he was not happy about it, he really had no choice but to give in. So after yelling out to Gina and Rob and receiving no reply, we set off to the Allens' house.

The lights were still on although it was quite late.

As we trooped through the front door a voice whispered, 'Shh! Fiona is in bed.'

'Hey, it's me,' Scotchie shouted. 'Got some mates with me.'

'Scott, I've told you a million times before – keep your voice down!'

We found both his parents sitting in the lounge room, with the TV on low.

'Hello, Mr Allen. My name's Andy,' my brother began as Scotchie made no move to introduce us. 'That's Lucy.'

The stepfather slowly looked up from his newspaper and examined Andy through thick heavy glasses. 'It's not Mr Allen, boy, it's Mr Thornycroft.'

Having corrected my brother, he snapped the paper back in front of his face and continued reading. Andy sank into a nearby chair while Mrs Thornycroft made us all a cup of tea. Soon we were awkwardly balancing cups and saucers on our laps.

'What are you watching on TV? Anything good?' Scotchie asked.

'There's been an excellent program on the ABC about the Swiss Alps. It's a shame that you weren't here to see it,' his mother replied, sipping her tea.

Scotchie grunted.

'We are all going to Switzerland next summer,' she told us.

'Wow, that's great!' Andy said, impressed.

Duncan came in and began to set up a chessboard on the polished side table. He and his stepfather settled into a serious, silent game of tactics.

'Are you going to the rest of Europe as well?' asked Andy.

'Yeah, we're gonna be dragged all around,' Scotchie muttered.

'As you can see, Scott would prefer not to go. He seems to think that his mind doesn't need broadening, nor that he needs to have many different experiences if he is to get on in the world.'

Scotchie grimaced and blew expert smoke rings into the air. His mother coughed pointedly, a short dry cough. Nobody knew what to say. I, for one, certainly didn't want to take sides in a family argument.

'Anyway, I expect that Rob has told you about his matriculation results?' Mrs Thornycroft continued.

'He hasn't mentioned anything to us,' I said. 'Although I'm sure that he's told Gina. So how did he go?'

'He got all A's. We're so proud of him.'

'That's fantastic!' I said.

Mrs Thornycroft smiled. 'Cake, anyone?' she asked, as she passed around some plates. 'And where do you live in town?'

'Prahran,' I replied, taking care not to drop any crumbs on the carpet.

'That's nice. I suppose that Scott has mentioned that we live in Eltham. It's a long way out of the city, but it really is like God's own paradise in the springtime. Mr Thornycroft says that he would like . . . Ah, there's Robert.' She smiled as we heard the front door close quietly.

'Hello, Mum. Any tea left in the pot?' Rob asked as he tiptoed into the room. 'Oh, you lot are here too,' he said, looking around at us with obvious surprise.

'Yes, but we're just going,' I said, quickly standing up. 'Hey, and congratulations to you for your great results!'

Rob acknowledged me with a nod.

'Lucy, it's been very nice to meet you. Scott is so naughty, you know. He doesn't usually let us meet his friends.' Mrs Thornycroft shook her head.

'Yeah, wonder why not,' Scotchie said under his breath.

'There's absolutely no need for insolence,' his stepfather boomed, glowering across the chessboard.

Mrs Thornycroft showed us to the door.

'Scott, see your friends to the gate. And make sure, for goodness sake, that you wear some shoes.' She disappeared into the kitchen to make Robert a fresh cup of tea.

We shuffled awkwardly in the doorway while Scotchie searched for a pair of shoes. After a minute and a quick glance over his shoulder, he leapt outside on his bare, dirty feet.

At the gate we waved a hurried goodbye and headed up the road. As we walked along in subdued silence, I thought of Scotchie back at that house. Somehow he just didn't seem to belong there.

EIGHT

It had been a real scorcher, one of those days when you could see the heat rising off the sand, a beautiful day spent lazing around on the beach and then riding the horses along the shoreline at dusk. It seemed such a shame that the summer holidays had to end in a few days' time.

As usual Scotchie came over that night, but he was strangely restless. Eventually he dragged me outside to wander aimlessly up and down the road before he decided to sit down under the only street light. We rested our backs against the wooden pole, listening to the distant roar of the sea. I watched the moths overhead pounding against the neon beam while Scotchie just stared into space.

Suddenly we were surrounded by darkness. The street lamp had gone out. I blinked and examined the stars, which now appeared so much brighter.

'It must be midnight, when all the street lights automatically turn off,' I said.

'S'pose so.'

Our voices seemed to echo in the inky night. I looked up at the small sliver of a moon.

'It's incredible to think that there were people actually walking around on that moon just six months ago,' I remarked.

There was no reply.

'Well, isn't it?'

'It's bloody disgraceful!' Scotchie snapped. 'What a goddamn waste of money! It cost a fortune and yet there's still such misery on Earth. Why didn't the Americans just hand the money over to India instead?'

I turned to look at him but couldn't see his face.

'Scotchie?'

'Yeah?'

'Tell me a story.'

'Stuff that for a joke!' Then I heard him sigh. 'Oh, all right. What about?'

'I don't know. Anything.'

'Well . . . once upon a time there was a beautiful girl with long brown hair and stunning grey eyes. She had a holiday house near the beach. One day she met a—'

'Hey! I don't think I like this story.'

'You're so bloody fussy. Okay, here's another one . . . Once upon a time there was a young boy who had a very special pet sheep called Dags. Every day he'd take Dags for a long walk and tell him all about his problems. They were best mates for years. For Dags was a black sheep, you see, just like the boy. Probably the only one in his family too.' Scotchie gave a hollow laugh.

'So what happened to Dags?'

Scotchie hesitated for a moment before saying bitterly, 'An arsehole neighbour shot him. Apparently Dags was getting into his veggie garden or something. The boy went berserk and wanted to kill the bastard, but of course he didn't. He just cried a bit in his room . . . probably.'

We both watched a shooting star fall and fade from sight.

'What did the boy do then?' I asked, hoping to change the subject.

'Well, as he grew up he decided that he didn't like school much and I guess his school didn't particularly like him either. So after fifth form, he headed off to Dookie Agricultural College to study farming. He did extremely well there because it was exactly what he wanted to do. He bought some land way up in the bush as well as a mean black dog called Fang, and together they lived in a beautiful run-down old shack.'

'Yes, but wasn't he lonely out there?'

'Nah, not him! He had Fang, didn't he? I guess though he did finally get married, but not till he was at least thirty, maybe even thirty-five. He just played around a lot till then. Besides, he didn't have heaps of time for that sort of thing 'cos he was working hard on other important stuff. Before he knew it, he'd become incredibly famous and everyone came from miles around to see the great man. And you should've seen his mum's face!'

'But what exactly was he famous for?' I asked, confused by the end of the story. There was a pause, filled only by the buzzing of the electrical wires overhead.

'How the hell should I goddamn know what he was famous for?' Scotchie yelled.

'Okay, okay. Calm down. Tell me what this guy did after he became famous.'

But Scotchie was not to be eased back into his story this time.

'He went back to school! That's what he bloody well did! Shit! Do you realise that we've only got four days left? Then it's back to prison where you're locked up for another crappy year.'

'Prison? School isn't that bad. Actually, I'm looking forward to fourth form and starting German,' I said.

Scotchie groaned. 'Let me explain something to you – fourth form is no better than third form. In fact, school gets worse

29

the higher up you go. Sure, they try to sell it to you more the older you get, by giving you bribes like Economics and bloody German. But all the time the bastards are strangling you with school ties, homework and rules! "Thou shalt not swear, thou shalt not drink, thou shalt not do anything that is fun" . . .' He lit a cigarette angrily and I watched the match fly up in the air before it went out.

'You're being ridiculous,' I said. 'My school isn't like that at all.'

'Lucy, you are such an unbelievable little suck!'

I grabbed a handful of dirt and dumped it on his head. He twisted around, grabbed me and flattened me to the ground. The smell of his sheepskin jacket was strong as he leant his face over mine.

'Get off, Scott! Now!' I ordered.

'Not till you kiss me I won't!' He sounded dangerously close.

'Well then, we'll be here all year, won't we?'

'Shit! Why are you so bloody unfriendly all the time?' Scotchie muttered and released me.

'And why are you such a sex maniac?'

'You're wasting your time learning German. What you need to study is good old sex education.' He took off up the road.

'Well, we don't have that at our school,' I shouted after him.

'Ha! You don't say!'

I spun around and went to kick the lamppost, but decided against it. Fuming, I marched off home instead.

NINE

Pack-up day arrived. It was always the worst day by far out of the whole holidays. The cat, as usual, went missing and the dog spent the entire day in the car, just in case we forgot to pack him at the last minute.

Naturally my mother fussed around, frantically trying to clean up the house. Andy and my father went to the tip, arguing all the way there and all the way back. Meanwhile Gina and I rode the horses over to the farm where they lived for most of the year and then added to the general chaos.

Just as I was helping my father load the trailer, Scotchie and Richard came wandering up.

'G'day, Doc! Need anything?' Scotchie asked.

'Sure, go and grab the large spanner from the shed.'

He disappeared but returned empty-handed a few minutes later. 'Sorry, it's not there.'

Dad went off to search for it.

'Lucy – catch!' Scotchie threw a small package across to me.

I looked at the present, which was wrapped in pink toilet paper. It felt slightly wet. Richard was grinning at me as I tore off the sticky tape. An ice cube was all there was inside.

'Well, how do you like it?' Scotchie asked.

'Um, it's . . . it's a bit of ice,' I replied, puzzled.

'Lucy, you win the iceblock award of the summer for being so damn frigid,' he said with a wink at Richard.

I just stared at him. Richard by now was doubled up with laughter.

'It's a joke, Joyce!' Scotchie explained, grinning.

'Who's Joyce?' asked John, who had just arrived.

Scotchie came over to where I was standing, still speechless. 'Okay, so I'm a sore loser,' he admitted quietly.

I finally knew what to say. 'And here's a little something for you too, you bastard!'

I grabbed the neck of his T-shirt and dropped the ice cube down his front. Scotchie fished it out and ate it, crunching it up loudly. His clown routine made me laugh, in spite of myself.

'See you round, mate!' he said, grinning into my face. He then turned away and headed towards the gate with Richard.

'Bye,' John mumbled and patted me on the shoulder.

I watched the three of them saunter up the road. Scotchie was slouching along, his hands in his pockets, while Richard strode alongside him. John was already way behind. My father came out of the house, carrying an esky.

'Lucy, bring out the rest of those boxes. Come on, it's getting late.'

I took one last look at the disappearing sheepskin jacket.

Inside the fridge was turned off and the curtains were drawn. Andy found the cat and put him in the car. The summer holidays were over for another year.

TEN

Wearing a newly ironed dress and short socks to show off my suntan, I went back to school. Although I didn't admit it very often, I enjoyed school. The work never gave me much trouble and so there was always plenty of time left over to talk to my friends. That first week of term, my best friend Sarah and I managed to swap hundreds of holiday stories in whispers at the back of the classroom. Naturally I told her about Scotchie, but somehow never got around to telling her about my iceblock award.

Anyway, fourth form was the important year at my school for there was dancing class. It was held in a huge hall and lots of teenagers from other private schools attended as well. Mainly old-fashioned dancing was taught, but really I don't think anyone actually learnt how to waltz. For us girls, dancing class meant only one thing: the fifth-form boys who were there, and as we went to an all-girls school, this was enough of a reason to go.

Only three girls out of my class didn't bother to sign up; I wasn't one of them. Suddenly I found myself caught up in a whirl of new dresses, make-up and teenage magazines . . . along with everyone else. Mondays and Tuesdays were spent discussing the dancing class of the previous Saturday night. Thursdays and Fridays we talked about what we were all going to wear on the following Saturday. On Wednesdays the conversations merged somewhere between the past and the future.

Saturdays were for hair washing, last-minute trips to buy stockings in the morning and in the evening there was always the two-hour long session of putting on make-up. For all of us, dancing class was the proving ground for social success. Accordingly, we agonised over it.

Sometimes there were parties, which presented even greater trauma, and greater excitement, for then it was important to go with a boy. Generally I was lucky.

Occasionally Scotchie would turn up at these parties, accompanied by a gang of mates, although he never actually ventured inside. When he'd first see me, his blue eyes would light up and he'd never fail to mess up my carefully arranged hair. I'd stay outside for a while chatting with him. But if a girl in a miniskirt walked past alone, Scotchie would move away from me and call out, 'Hey, honey, do you wanna come home and check out my bedspread?'

He told me that he often got to score. Frankly, I found it extremely embarrassing to be with him when he behaved like that. I'd beg him to come inside, but never with any success. He seemed to prefer hanging around in the front yard on the dark outskirts of the party. Eventually I'd give up on him, redo my hair (while Scotchie looked on laughing) and head indoors to join the others who were dancing under the coloured lights. After all, I wanted to fit into the 'social scene' (as he sneeringly called it) even if he didn't.

My friends were always quick to ask, 'Lucy, who on earth was that creep you were talking to?' Probably Scotchie's friends didn't think much of me either.

Still, it was great to see him even if we did now seem to live in two different worlds.

From time to time I'd receive news about him from Rob via Gina. But when they split up and the bulletins stopped, it was really no great loss, as I could never trust Rob's reports anyway. So Scotchie and I drifted even further apart.

I guess he became increasingly busy with his own life. I know I did. As the year progressed, I found that I needed to study harder than I'd ever done before. I stopped going to parties and devoted all my energy to staying on top of my schoolwork. A couple of times I went to my best friend Sarah's holiday house in Portsea for intensive study weekends. In December I sat each exam in turn and discovered that my hard work had paid off. My results were excellent. With an enormous sense of relief, I packed away my school uniform for another year. The summer holidays had finally arrived and with them came a boyfriend.

Neil entered my life with a surfboard tucked under one arm. His family had just bought a beach house near ours at Shoreham. He was very good-looking, with broad shoulders and gorgeous curly blond hair. I spent a lot of the summer sitting on my beach towel, catching glimpses of him surfing and waiting for him to come in from the waves. Luckily Gina had given me *War and Peace* for Christmas. Sometimes a shadow would fall across the page and I'd look up to find John. We'd talk for ages. John was at a bit of a loose end with Scotchie still overseas with his family, and besides, I always enjoyed catching up with him.

All too soon, the holidays ended. Neil locked up his surfboard in the shed, went back to his far-away suburb and never got around to telephoning as he said he would.

As for me, I returned to school and launched headlong into fifth form, and arrangements for the all-important school dance.

ELEVEN

But suddenly, dramatically, the roll of days stopped. Everything fell apart with a crash. On 4 April 1971 my father had a heart attack and was rushed to hospital. That night, as he lay in intensive care, we waited for news. I stayed in my room but couldn't cry, finding it impossible to believe what had just happened. Somehow I went to sleep and woke up the next morning to hear that he would probably be all right. So mechanically I got ready for school. My mother made my lunch, just as she did every morning, and I caught the usual bus.

At the school entrance, I ran into Sarah.

'Hi! Did you do that History homework? Wasn't it dreadful?'

'No. Er, my father . . . he had a heart attack last night,' I replied, my voice sounding as if it didn't belong to me.

'Oh. Is he okay?'

'We think so.' My hand tightened over the straps of my schoolbag.

'That's good.' Sarah paused for a minute. 'Well, I finished the whole assignment. It was difficult and I had a lot of trouble with the fifth question which . . .'

She raved on and on, but I was no longer listening. My whole head felt as though it was going to explode and yet my best friend didn't seem to notice that anything was wrong. Or maybe she didn't know what to say. I made some excuse and left her.

I don't know why my friends didn't help me. Perhaps they did try but from where I was standing, it certainly didn't feel as though they did. My father began to improve very slowly, however, the shock still remained, trapped inside me. Each lunchtime the other girls would take one look at my face and immediately take flight, leaving me alone to stare miserably at my sandwich.

I suppose I did manage, but really, I had little choice, for Gina had moved out to attend university a month earlier, which meant that I was the eldest one at home. My mother had taken it all very badly. I tried to comfort her, but she wanted her husband at home with her. A healthy husband. There was nothing I could do except be brave myself. When I dragged myself off to school in the morning, I guess I looked around for somebody to support me, but found no one.

One afternoon I came home and was heading up the stairs to my room when my mother called out to tell me that I had a visitor. I threw down my schoolbag and went into the sitting room. To my astonishment, there was Scotchie.

'G'day.'

'What! You're wearing shoes!' I exclaimed.

He'd changed. Now sixteen, he was much better looking and had grown even taller. He'd filled out a lot too.

There was an awkward pause while we just stood in the middle of the room, looking at each other. My mother picked up her book and disappeared.

'Hey, Lucy, I'm really sorry about your old man,' Scotchie whispered.

Suddenly my whole body went rigid. I rammed my eyes shut, desperately trying to control a flood of tears. My insides were tearing, churning. I was struggling to breathe. I opened my eyes to find Scotchie watching me. He reached out and pulled me gently to his chest, holding me close. I fell apart completely.

'I don't want Dad to die,' I sobbed, the tears running in torrents down my cheeks.

'Lucy, he's going to be okay,' Scotchie soothed. 'He's getting better and he'll be home soon.'

'Yes but . . . he almost died,' I wept. 'Scotchie . . .' I tried to tell him how I felt, but I couldn't.

He sighed, stroking my hair. 'I know,' he murmured.

I looked up into his sad face. I remembered those long sessions when Scotchie and my father debated world issues around the barbecue at Shoreham. I began to cry again, but this time I felt the warmth of his arms comforting me.

Eventually my father was allowed home. He wandered around the house in a dressing-gown, looking lost. He'd had a fright and it was not an easy lesson to forget – not for any of us. Andy withdrew into the sanctity of his bedroom, rarely to be seen, while my mother spent her time panicking over the slightest little thing. As for me, every night I would rest my head against my father's chest just to reassure myself that his heart was still beating. Each of us, privately, lived in fear.

But Scotchie helped me survive through those traumatic weeks. He rang up constantly and I was always pleased to see his face at the door. He had stepped back into my life just when I needed someone. He listened with concern to all of my troubles and sometimes, in the end, even managed to make me smile. In fact, I don't know how I would have coped without him.

In May my father returned to work and our lives should have gone back to normal. However, it was then that my mother became the problem.

'Quickly!' she'd hiss at me. 'Look in the pockets of your father's coat and see if there are any cigarettes!'

Dad had been ordered by his doctor to stop smoking, once and for all. He was finding this exceedingly difficult and Mum's nagging was making it even harder. I refused to do her bidding and cringed at the way she shrieked when she caught my father having an occasional puff. Whereas previously there had scarcely been a cross word between them, now my parents began to argue constantly.

To make matters worse, my mother started to lean heavily on me for support. She raved to me for hours about all kinds of crap, as if I had suddenly become her best buddy. One night I was so fed up that I wrote a poem, all about how much I hated her. Admittedly it wasn't a good poem, certainly not one of my finest, but it did help me release some of the anger I was feeling. It was full of the F word. Unfortunately the next day it fell out of my folder at school and someone handed it in.

Straight away the school went into overdrive to find out who had written the dreadful poem. The handwriting was quickly traced and my parents were instantly summoned into the headmistress's office. I was mortified. Mum read the poem quietly and, to my complete amazement, understood why I'd written it. She forgave me immediately. But the headmistress didn't, even though she was not the one under attack.

After that scene in the office at school, my mother and I settled into a new understanding of each other. Perhaps she stopped pressuring me so much or maybe I saw her in a new light; I'm not sure, but whatever happened, it was a major turning point. My problems shifted from home to school, and this time there was to be no reconciliation.

For it wasn't just the business over the poem. I had gone to a moratorium – a protest march against the war in Vietnam – and my absence from school that day had been noticed. When asked to explain why I'd been away, I told the truth. I was the only one in the whole school who had marched and admitted it.

Once again it was back to the headmistress's office. There was talk of expelling me but it was decided to give me one last chance. One last chance? With almost a hundred thousand people at the demonstration in Melbourne against the Vietnam War, I felt that I had done nothing wrong. I hadn't committed any terrible crime. In fact, it was just the opposite – I had done what every Australian should have done! Hell, I'd even gone to the demonstration with the approval of my parents and had marched alongside my sister!

Everyone at school knew about my poem and that I had marched. After years of satisfactory report cards and always fitting in, suddenly I found myself labelled a 'troublemaker' and a 'radical'. I was on the outside, and in a small school like mine, the outside was a horrible place to be. I could do nothing right. I was often publicly singled out as a bad example to the rest of the class and my 'friends' completely melted away.

My English teacher referred sneeringly to me as 'the left-wing member of the class'. I'd never been very political, but judgement had been passed and so I decided to live up to my teacher's expectations. At least being criticised for something you are is better than for something you're not, I decided. Scotchie happily lent me *The Little Red Schoolbook*, which I began reading under the cover of my desk. I guess it didn't help my reputation, but by that stage I figured it was past saving.

I suddenly understood what Scotchie had been trying to tell me a few summers ago under that lamppost. School was a prison, after all. I'd been working so hard at being accepted as an inmate that I simply hadn't realised it before.

Now Scotchie and I were both rattling the bars.

TWELVE

As time went on, I became increasingly miserable at school. One day, my parents watched me viciously kick my bag into a corner and slump dejectedly into a chair. They exchanged glances before sitting down on the couch. For weeks they'd seen my face as I came in through the door after school, but I guess they'd hoped that my troubles would eventually pass.

'Lucy, is it really as bad as that?' My mother's voice begged me to contradict her but I simply couldn't.

I just nodded. There was silence in the room.

Suddenly my father leapt to his feet. 'I think you'd better stay home for the rest of the week. After that, we'll work out some kind of plan.'

I waited for Mum to argue against this idea, but instead she said, 'Maybe you should go down to Shoreham. The peace and quiet might help, and it's a good place to rest for a while.'

So it was decided. My difficulties at school weren't over but at least I was to escape for four whole days. I felt relieved, too, that I'd finally made my parents understand the seriousness of the whole situation. I raced straight over to the telephone to ring up Scotchie to share the good news with him.

I caught two trains and a bus before finally making it to our beach house. I read a lot and spent hours walking out my feelings along the empty beach. On Friday night, after a meal of baked beans and eggs on toast, I stretched out on the rug in front of the fire. The night outside was very still, without even a breath of wind to stir the trees. Lazily I watched the flames flickering.

Suddenly there was a sound of feet and the front door burst open.

'G'day! Have ya missed me?'

'Scotchie! What are you doing here?'

I began to get up from the floor but he threw himself full length on top of me, pinning me down. His glowing eyes studied my face for a minute. Then he winked and said, 'Aha! I've got you alone at last! One whole weekend! Let's start right now by making it the dirtiest weekend on record!' His lips started to close in on mine.

'Not so fast, mister,' I replied, managing to throw him off. I stood up. 'But it is great to see you.'

'Nice way you have of showing it! I mean, a man hitchhikes all night, through rain, hail and whatever, only to be given the bloody cold shoulder. The big brush off.'

'Look, I just can't . . . It isn't . . .'

There was an awkward pause, until I broke the silence with a laugh.

'Is it safe now?' I asked, walking back over to him.

'Wait a minute,' he answered and put his hands behind his back with an exaggerated flourish. 'Yeah, you're safe.'

I sat down beside him. 'So what's been happening?'

'You know how I always change my school tie when I want to smoke on the train home? Well, last Wednesday arvo—'

'What? I didn't know you were still smoking. Since when?' I interrupted.

But Scotchie just rolled his eyes and continued his story, 'Anyway, last Wednesday I'd left my usual selection of ties in the locker and so all I could find was my mate's one from his Catholic school. So I slipped it on and lit up a fag. According to my mate, there was a huge commotion in assembly the next day about some scruffy kid with dirty shoes who was seen smoking on the four forty-five train to Eltham. Ha!'

'Schools certainly make a big deal over nothing,' I said sourly as I put another log onto the fire.

'Sure do.'

Scotchie got up to play a Bob Dylan record on the stereo. Sitting back down again on the floor he ripped off his sandshoes and threw them into a corner of the room.

'And how have you been, Lucy?'

'Okay, I guess,' I sighed. 'School has really been getting me down. I don't fit in there any more.'

'That's 'cos it's a conservative, fascist hell-hole, like all private schools. Shit! I've never been accepted at my school,' Scotchie said cheerfully (even proudly I thought). 'Why don't you switch schools and go to a high school? That's where the real kids go, you know.'

I mulled over this new idea. 'You could be right.'

'Anyway, by the end of this year, I'm gonna be free! I reckon that I might go to Dookie Agricultural College next year and become a farmer – that is, if the old lady lets me. Hey, quiet for a minute! It's my favourite song.'

Scotchie began to sing along to 'Blowin' in the Wind'. When the track ended he said quietly, 'Lucy?'

'Yes?'

'Do you ever think about death?'

I gazed into the fire. 'A lot, especially since my father's heart attack.'

'Why the hell do we live if we're just going to die? What's the point? Why are we born if we're only going to be food for the worms at the end?' Scotchie's eyes blazed.

'I don't know.'

'Ever think about suicide?'

'Sure. Who doesn't? But it would be incredibly hard for my parents to handle.'

'Huh!' Scotchie snorted. 'My mother would throw a party if I killed myself.'

'Don't be stupid!' I scolded, playing with the collar of his faded denim jacket.

'Sometimes when I'm in my old car burning around the paddock, I think that if I just smacked into a tree, it'd be instant curtains for me. How easy that would be.'

Suddenly he grinned at me.

'Sex is like dying, you know,' he suggested hopefully.

'No thanks,' I replied firmly, and took my hands off his collar.

'Oh.'

Scotchie piled some cushions under his head and lay down on the floor, stretching his feet out over the hearth. Eventually I lay down too. After many attempts to smother me and just as many shouted protests, we finally drifted off to sleep as the sun was beginning to rise.

Saturday and Sunday passed far too quickly. We ate heaps of pies, had running races along the beach and I tried to bury Scotchie in the sand. But finally, sadly, we had to go home.

When I arrived back, alone, my mother met me at the door.

'Hello, dear. How did it go?'

'Oh, just great. Perfect in fact. It was so good to get away. Thanks heaps, Mum, for letting me go,' I said as I made myself some toast.

'You certainly had nice weather for it. By the way, have the gutters on the sunroom been fixed?'

'Sorry, I didn't notice.'

She turned away and started to leave the kitchen.

'Er, Mum, Scott Allen came down to stay too.'

'Did he now?' She spun around to face me, eyes searching mine. 'Well, I suppose you weren't lonely.'

'We had such a fantastic time together. Yesterday Scotchie fell in the creek; you should've seen him, Mum!'

Her face relaxed into a smile.

'I'm glad you had a good time. I worry sometimes,' she said quietly. She locked the back door before adding, 'Mrs Thornycroft rang on Friday night to tell me where Scott was. But you know, dear, I always trust you to do the right thing. Anyway, don't forget to turn out the lights.' She touched me lightly on the arm and left the room. 'Goodnight.'

I ran my fingers through my hair. I was really glad that I'd told her about Scotchie.

THIRTEEN

Scotchie was now a frequent visitor to our place, but only on a Saturday or a Sunday. Weekdays we had to make do with telephone calls.

'Lucy, will you get off that phone? I want to use it,' Andy was always complaining.

At almost fourteen my brother was still a brat. He liked to pretend that he had a girlfriend (which he didn't), whom he was just about to ring (which he wasn't). He only played this game when Scotchie and I were on the phone. In actual fact, he was jealous. He didn't like his hero hanging around his sister.

My father wasn't ecstatic about the new arrangement either, but he generally used a different excuse to shorten our chats.

'Is she still talking to Scott? I've explained to her before that one of my patients might be trying to ring. I can't have the line busy all the time,' he yelled down the passage.

'I'll only be a minute longer, Dad,' I shouted back before whispering into the mouthpiece, 'Scotchie, I've got to go. My father's off his head – severe nicotine withdrawal.'

'Hang on! I've forgotten to tell you something. Rob and . . .'

We heard the phone in the other room being picked up and the sound of breathing. 'Hello? Hello?'

'G'day, Doc. We're just finishing, okay?'

'Hang up now!'

There was the thud of a phone being slammed down.

'Hell, your old man isn't in a good mood tonight, is he? Anyway,' continued Scotchie, 'Rob, me and John are driving down to the beach this weekend. Wanna come along?'

'You don't think Rob would mind if I went too?' I hesitated.

'Why would he?'

Suddenly my father appeared. 'Time to say goodbye,' he ordered.

I just managed to get in, 'Great idea. See you,' before he cut us off. My father thundered out of the room.

It was difficult to persuade my parents into letting me go away for the weekend, especially my father. Certainly he liked Scotchie a lot, but when this same boy was involved with his daughter . . . well, that was another matter entirely. However, they did at last agree. I think what convinced them was the fact that Rob and John would be there as well, although I didn't believe for one moment that their presence would make the slightest difference to Scotchie's behaviour. Still, I didn't argue with my parents' logic.

And so that Friday evening, I found myself in the car heading down to the Allen family's beach house. On the way we stopped for fish and chips. John and Scotchie jumped out of the car to place the order, leaving Rob and me alone. After an awkward silence, he asked, 'How's your sister going? She's studying at Monash Uni, isn't she?'

'Gina's always busy. Her history course involves a lot of essays, or that's what she tells us at any rate. You don't run into her at uni?'

He shook his head. 'I'm at Melbourne so our paths never cross.'

'We don't see her very often. She's living in a house with friends, I'm not sure where exactly. And she's involved with some political group.'

'Oh? What kind?'

'A socialist party, I believe.'

'That figures!' Rob muttered.

The topic clearly closed, he then stared fixedly at the steering wheel until the others returned.

Later on that night, we were still hungry. Somebody suggested making a cake and so we upended the kitchen in our hunt for a recipe book. Failing to find one, we decided to make up the recipe as we went along.

'Eggs! We don't have any eggs,' grumbled John, who seemed to be very practical.

'We don't need eggs,' said Scotchie, climbing over the table to get the butter off the bench.

'Get off the table!' shouted Rob. 'Heaven knows where your smelly feet have been!'

'What do you mean smelly?' Scotchie shoved a sandshoe under his brother's nostrils.

'Why on earth can't you learn how to behave?'

'Hey! Are we going to make this cake or not?' I said.

'Right! Mixing bowl?' John asked, looking around.

'Mixing bowl!' repeated Scotchie as he threw one across the room like a frisbee. Fortunately John caught it. 'Mixing spoon?'

A spoon hurtled onto the table. Several ingredients were dumped into the bowl and Scotchie began madly stirring. Finally the mixture was poured into a cake tin.

'This should take half an hour in the oven,' John told us. He'd taken charge of the whole operation. 'What's the time now?'

'Don't know. The clock has stopped. Hang on a minute,' said Rob and went into the next room. 'At the third stroke it will be eleven twenty precisely,' he called, as he hung up the phone.

Exactly thirty minutes (and eight phone calls) later, John opened the oven door. We all craned to have a look.

'Bloody hell! What happened?' Scotchie groaned.

It didn't even look like a cake. There was the mixture that we had put into the tin, only now it was hard as a rock. John examined the empty flour packet.

'Well, there's your problem right there,' he muttered. 'Plain flour. We should have used self-raising.'

We tried to eat the 'cake' but it tasted really terrible. At least Rob found a large packet of stale chips at the back of a cupboard and so our stomachs felt vaguely satisfied by the time we went to bed.

Scotchie and I got into a single bed in the back bedroom. We lay together looking out at the night sky. Scotchie reached for my hand and held it gently.

'Great night, eh?' he whispered.

I ran my fingers over his hand and I sensed that he was smiling at me through the darkness. We kissed for a while.

'So how's about it?' he asked, pressing himself up hard against me.

'How about what?'

'You know.'

'No!'

'Why not?'

'Just no. By the way, how's that economics essay going?' I asked, hoping to change the subject.

'It's not.'

'Whoops, sorry for asking.'

Scotchie sat up and switched on the light.

'Actually, I reckon I'm going to fail HSC.'

'With your brains? Not a chance! Anyway, you've still got three months to go until the final exams.'

'That's nothing,' he said. 'Just wait till you're in HSC next year. The pressure really gets you down. You're meant to just work, work, work.'

'Who says that – the school?'

'Yeah, and it's true if you want to pass.'

'Scotchie, you can only do your best,' I said and then wished that I hadn't used such a boring cliché.

'But what if that isn't good enough?' he cried. 'Brilliant Duncan is a Rhodes Scholar at Oxford. Robert is doing exceptionally well in his honours degree at Melbourne Uni, of course. Even Fiona is captain of her class, again. Then there's Scott. Pity about him!'

He flung back the blankets.

'The old lady is on my back the whole time. She expects her youngest son to be just as wonderful as the others,' Scotchie continued bitterly.

'So? Since when have you obeyed your mother?'

He laughed and fell silent for a while. Then he said quietly, 'My father died before he was thirty-five. He'd done nothing in his life. Sure, he'd had a few kids and had set up a business, but that's about it. I don't want to die like that, wondering if I've wasted my life. It's not just a matter of exam results and a bloody career. Hell, I know that school sucks. But . . . There's a whole world out there that stinks. Sometimes I want to pick the entire crappy thing up and shake it, and know that it will never be the same again. Then I reckon that I could die, satisfied that I'd done something to fix that huge goddamn mess.' Scotchie sighed before adding, 'Yeah, I guess I want to be exceptional too. But I'm kind of frightened, in case I don't make it.'

'You'll get there,' I said, totally certain of this. 'You'll see.'

We lay down again and I stroked his back gently. Scotchie had obviously exhausted himself and gradually the tension seemed to drop away from his body. The stillness deepened. He turned over towards me and I could feel his wild hair brushing against my cheek as we settled into sleep.

The next morning I woke up before him, watching him sleep and remembering the agonised words he had spoken under the cover of night. He seemed so confused, caught between hitting out at the world and yet wanting to be an important part of it all. I sighed, wishing that somehow he shared the same confident vision of his future that I had.

Suddenly he grunted and blinked drowsily at me. Then he sat up and began to sing, very softly, his current favourite Bob Dylan song.

'This must be the day that all of my dreams come true

'So happy just to be alive

'Underneath the sky of blue.'

He grinned and winked at me, before singing the chorus at the top of his voice.

'On this new mornin', new morning

'On this new mornin' with you.'

'Shut up! I'm trying to sleep!' Rob called from the next room.

Scotchie immediately leapt out of bed, grabbed a pillow and ran into Rob's room. Shouting and sounds of fighting followed. I could hear John's tired voice telling them to stop.

I got up and wandered into the kitchen to put the kettle on for coffee.

FOURTEEN

To tell you the truth, I really don't know exactly when it was that I fell in love with Scotchie, for there were no blazing fireworks or slow-motion running into each other's arms. It wasn't like that at all. I guess that love kind of grew, while I wasn't looking.

One night I was in bed and, as usual, I was thinking about Scotchie. I remembered how good it felt to be kissing, and lying beside him, as if I belonged there. The memory of our closeness unsettled me and I switched on the light. My decision had been made.

My mother was alone in the sitting room, reading, so I flopped into a nearby chair and brought my knees up under my chin.

'Mum?'

'Yes?'

'I've decided . . . er, is Andy in bed?'

She put down her book and gave me her full attention.

'What is it, dear?'

'I was thinking . . . you've always said that you trust us kids to do the right thing,' I began nervously.

She nodded, waiting.

'That you trust our judgement?'

'Lucy, you know I do. Now, what's the problem?'

'I am sixteen, after all.'

This time my mother didn't encourage me to continue. Perhaps she knew what was coming.

'I . . . I want to go on the Pill,' I blurted out in a rush of bravery.

'Oh.'

There was silence. I forced myself to look at my mother, straight in the eyes. It felt as if the whole world had suddenly emptied, leaving only the tension between us. I didn't know what else to say; I'd said it all.

'I'm not sure that's a good idea,' my mother finally began. 'The Pill isn't something that a girl of your age should take because your body hasn't finished developing yet. And then there's another issue . . . No, listen to me for just for a moment,' she continued as I opened my mouth to speak. 'You mightn't realise it now, but once you start having sex . . .'

I looked down at the carpet, wishing that we could stay on the subject of the Pill. It was far less embarrassing than to discuss the actual sex part of the equation. My mother went on, 'You won't be able to go back to simply holding hands with your next boyfriend.'

I glared at her. 'There won't be a next boyfriend. I'm going to stay with Scotchie.'

'At your age, you really can't know that for sure.'

'I really, really love him,' I explained and studied the pattern on the carpet again.

'I'm sure you do.'

'Well then, it's the right thing.'

'I don't know, dear. It's hard for me to . . . It's just that . . .' Her voice trailed off.

I wondered what she was trying to say, but I couldn't work it out. She never gave me many clues as to what she really felt.

It must be hard to be a parent sometimes, I thought. For my mother would remember me as a baby, a soft warm tiny baby to hold in her arms. And yet here I was now, that same daughter, asking for the Pill. It must be pretty strange, I decided.

Suddenly her voice, calm and steady, broke the silence. She'd obviously made up her mind.

'What would you do if I don't agree?' she asked.

'I guess I'd go to a doctor behind your back.'

'Or get pregnant,' she sighed. 'So what choice do I have?'

She got out of her chair and turned to me. 'I'll make an appointment with Dr Walsh. I don't want to take you to your father's surgery. In fact, I don't think we should tell him anything about this. I know it's the seventies, but he doesn't yet understand that his youngest daughter has grown up. He needs his little Lucy a bit longer.'

My mother smiled sadly at me and slowly left the room.

I jumped up, feeling waves of relief wash over me. It was only when I got back into bed that I realised how understanding my mother had been. After all, she could have ordered me not to sleep with Scotchie or even never to see him again. I was lucky that I had a mother like mine, I thought. Yet I had felt so relieved at closing the awkward topic that I had completely forgotten to thank her. Still, it was too late now, I decided, and switched off the light.

Two days later my mother and I went to see Dr Walsh. As for Scotchie, I told him nothing. I wanted to keep my options open, without totally committing myself just yet. We continued on as usual until one weekend, when I was allowed to go down to Shoreham with Scotchie.

All Friday night I felt extremely apprehensive and so kept pushing him away from me. Finally we lay, not touching at all. Both of us gazed out of the window. It was raining heavily. Scotchie had at last given up.

'Hey, what's wrong with you tonight? Or is it me?' he whispered.

'No, there's no problem, not really.'

'So why don't you want to kiss me?'

'I've been thinking. Scotchie, do you love me?'

'You know I do, stupid. How many thousands of times do I need to say it before I convince you?' He kissed me lightly on the nose.

'But how much do you love me?' I persisted.

'HEAPS!'

'Then why are you always leaping on top of me, without worrying if . . . well, I could get pregnant and you don't seem to care.'

'Of course I care,' he shouted, 'but I thought that you'd go on the Pill. That's what all the girls I know do.'

'Great! Thanks a lot!' Now I was yelling. I turned on the light and sat up, glaring down at him. 'Leave it all up to us, why don't you! You just have your fun and let us girls worry about that sort of thing.'

'Listen, Lucy, I've tried the other stuff. I reckon that the Pill is the best and I'm afraid that I can't take that. It's up to you.'

'But you haven't even bothered to talk about it.'

'Neither have you.'

'But I'm not the one who's always hassling to get into bed!' I punched the pillow.

Scotchie flung himself out of bed, threw on his denim jacket and stormed out of the room. I heard the toilet flush and the fridge door being opened. He came back, glass of milk in hand.

'Lucy, I know that I've kept pushing. But you're never willing to talk about anything related to sex. All you ever say is that it's not the right time. Finito. Well, that's pretty tough on me, 'cos I really want you. But of course it's your decision and I accept that.' He shrugged his shoulders. Settling himself back into bed, he added, 'So, do you want to talk about it? This whole contraception business, I mean?'

'No, I don't,' I answered and snapped off the light.

Together we examined the night sky.

'Scotchie?'

'Yeah?'

'Do you love me?'

'Shit!'

Neither of us spoke for ages. Then I finally managed to say, 'Guess what? Er, I'm on the Pill.'

I heard a long groan.

'You do realise that it's taken till three o'clock in the morning for you to tell me that? After all the arguing, I'm just too worn out to do anything about it.' Scotchie immediately rolled over to face the wall.

However, it wasn't long before he turned back and gently twisted my nose.

'I love you, but sometimes you drive me completely crazy.' He smiled into my face. Then he whispered, 'By the way, I'm not really too tired.'

FIFTEEN

'**W**ell? What was it like?' asked my friend Helen, who lived five doors up from us in Prahran. We were walking to the local milk bar on the following Wednesday afternoon.

'What on earth are you talking about?'

'You know, Lucy. Having sex with Scotchie, of course,' she persisted.

I flicked some dog hair off my school jumper and just grinned at her. We continued our walk in silence. At the shop, we bought a couple of ice-creams, and as we wandered slowly home, I said, 'Actually, it was fantastic.'

'Yes?'

But I couldn't tell her any more than that. The experience was still too close, too new even to know what to say. I needed time to sort the whole thing out in my head first. It was kind of personal, after all.

'I'll tell you later, okay?'

Helen smiled back, knowing that I would keep my promise.

It was rather strange the way the world seemed somehow different. I began to notice certain things more, like nighties. Every evening I'd change and get into bed just as I had done for years. But suddenly I became aware of the annoying way my nightie twisted around my body when I rolled over and so I'd have to take it off before I could fall sleep. After a while, I didn't bother putting one on at all.

It wasn't long before my mother started buying me presents. I often came home from school to find a package on my bed. She'd tell me that she was just passing a lingerie shop and there was a sale on . . . Sure enough, it would be a new nightie. My mother might have helped me go on the Pill, but she was obviously not ready to accept that things were no longer the same. So I took the hint. From then on, when I remembered, I took a folded nightie out of my drawer, carefully crumpled it and put it straight into the laundry basket. It did the trick and the flood of presents stopped.

My classmates, too, appeared in a different light. One day I watched a group of girls, my ex-friends, minutely examine each other's hair for split ends and I noticed for the first time that they were all blonde, of one shade or another. I listened as their conversation turned to who had their own Myer account card and who had to borrow their mother's, until I simply couldn't stand it any longer.

'Do you realise,' I interrupted, 'that our school has no scholarship program?'

'Meaning?' asked Mandy.

'Only girls from families that can afford the exorbitant school fees are able to come here.'

'So why is this a problem?'

'Why would we want to let just anybody into our school?' asked Sarah. 'Surely we have to be careful not to let our standards drop.'

'You don't understand,' I said. 'Scholarships are for clever girls. For example, there's a girl I know at Shoreham who is . . .'

'Where's Shoreham?' interrupted Jenny. 'I've never heard of the place.'

'Oh, it's on the other side of the peninsula from Portsea,' Marion explained.

I stood there, gobsmacked. I could hardly believe that I had been friends with such stuck-up little snobs for all those years.

That day I threw away my school gloves, vowing that I would leave and go to the local high school, no matter what. I knew that this would mean a big battle with my parents, because it was the 'alma mater' of both my mother and my aunt, and of course Gina had gone there as well. But I was absolutely determined.

Naturally Scotchie agreed with my decision to change schools. He himself had been expelled, after he was caught smoking on the train home, although he was allowed back to sit his final exams. In the meantime, he was now happily ensconced at home with his 'head down and bum up' – as he put it.

Mrs Thornycroft phrased it somewhat differently.

'Scott is engrossed in his studies at the moment,' she proudly informed me when she answered the phone one afternoon. 'He can't possibly be disturbed. Perhaps he can ring you back when he is ready for a break?'

'Hey, is that Lucy?' I heard Scotchie's voice in the background, before the sound of running feet. 'Lucy? You there or did the old lady cut us off?'

'Hi. I just wanted to know if you're missing me.'

'Like crazy.'

Our phone calls never lasted for less than an hour.

A few times I went to his place in Eltham for the weekend. It certainly wasn't as good as going to Shoreham, but as that was out of the question until after the exams were over, it was better than nothing. The taxi fare from Prahran to Eltham was enormous but Scotchie always waved my concerns away with a generous hand, as he signed it onto his stepfather's account card with the other.

The house was very impressive, made from mud bricks with high cathedral ceilings that were supported by huge wooden beams. There appeared to be lots of bedrooms, each with its own bathroom and study attached, and all had sliding glass doors that led onto a long balcony. From there, you could look out over the treed landscape and even glimpse the Yarra River winding its way through the bush. Downstairs, the formal dining room was full of silver dishes, all carefully arranged on the polished wooden sideboard. The library was adjacent, its walls covered with floor-to-ceiling bookcases and original paintings.

Scotchie's bedroom, too, had its share of paintings, but they were slapped together by a mate of his, and therefore unlikely ever to be valuable. Also competing for wall space were posters, mainly of Bob Dylan and Che Guevara. There was an enlarged photograph, slightly out of focus, of Dags, the black sheep he'd once had. Piles of dirty clothes were strewn everywhere and scrunched up paper littered the floor. On the bedside table was a book of poems by Wilfred Owen. Scotchie said that he liked to read it sometimes when he woke up.

One Sunday morning he did just that. Scotchie shouted 'Anthem for Doomed Youth' aloud, shaking his fist at me for added emphasis, as he and Owen raged against the futility of war. I tried to get him to be quiet, afraid that his parents would realise that he wasn't alone in his bed. He paused long enough to tell me that he was simply following his usual routine and continued reading. When he turned the page and began on 'The Next War', I got out of the small single bed. As I walked guiltily towards the guest room where I should have spent the night, I could still hear Scotchie's voice thundering down the passage.

Sunday lunch was a major event in that household, taking place straight after everyone's return from church. Although Scotchie had somehow been allowed to escape the local service, he was certainly not excused from the traditional lunch. Duncan, of course, was never there as he was still in England, but the rest of the family was expected to assemble at the table, unless they happened to be at Shoreham. Even Rob generally made it home for the day, despite the fact that he was now living in a college near Melbourne Uni.

This particular Sunday was no exception. Fiona set the table and Cooper the live-in housekeeper cooked the roast. The second-best crockery and cutlery sets were used, as well as the silver serviette rings.

At exactly twelve o'clock the two guests arrived. Mr and Mrs Bailey were obviously close friends of the Thornycrofts. Mr Bailey was a Member of Parliament for the Liberal Party and I wasn't told what his wife did.

We took our places around the table and the wine was soon poured.

'No thanks, Rob,' Scotchie said, covering his stemmed glass with his hand, 'I'd rather have a beer.' He got a stubby out of the fridge, took the top off and began to drink straight from the bottle.

Rob scowled at his brother and then addressed Mr Bailey. 'I was just wondering what you thought about the Liberal Party's chances of staying in power after the next election,' he remarked, to get the conversation going, I suppose.

'Well, lad, I think that they are extremely good. I don't think that we need to fear that radical Gough Whitlam – he will never amount to much.' Mr Bailey gave a little chuckle and everyone politely laughed with him.

'Yes, but you might have a bit of trouble over this Vietnam War business,' Mr Thornycroft put in.

'The newspapers do seem to be telling us that conscription is an important issue, especially for the younger voters,' his wife added.

Cooper placed the main course on the table.

'Who would like some gravy?' Scotchie asked and began to move the gravy boat down the table.

I looked at him in surprise. I had never known him to show such good manners.

'Oh, it's just a bunch of ratbags who are demonstrating in the streets over Vietnam,' Mr Bailey scoffed, helping himself to another slice of lamb.

'But there are tens of thousands of people who are marching – you surely can't ignore that. They can't all be "ratbags". And they strongly believe that Australia should have no part in the war,' Scotchie said in a steady, unfamiliar voice.

'Listen, when you get to my age you'll realise that war is inevitable and it's our duty to assist our military allies.' The politician smiled indulgently at him.

I held my breath and waited for an explosion. Didn't the man know how passionately anti-war Scotchie was? I watched Scotchie's hand tense around his stubby and yet he replied mildly, 'Perhaps my generation doesn't agree with you that war is inevitable.'

'Robert, please serve some more wine,' Mrs Thornycroft cut in and glanced coldly across the table at her youngest son.

'That's because they have never experienced a war on their doorstep,' Mr Bailey said. 'They have no idea what it's like.'

Scotchie hid his shaking hands under the cover of the tablecloth while his stepfather leant over and patted his friend on the arm.

'That's right,' Mr Thornycroft nodded. 'They simply don't realise. We beat the Germans and Japs in World War

Two and now we have to lend a hand in stamping out those communists.'

'Meanwhile we are killing countless innocent civilians, shooting them down like dogs as they run screaming in terror from the soldiers,' Scotchie muttered.

'It can't be helped,' Mr Thornycroft sighed.

Scotchie stared at his stepfather and then turned to his sister.

'That reminds me of a joke I heard the other day, although I've changed it a bit. How do you fit one hundred people into a Mini Minor?'

Fiona looked up expectantly.

'Make one a politician and the rest will crawl up his arse!'

His sister giggled nervously while elsewhere knives and forks were suspended in mid-air. Scotchie carefully folded his napkin, placed it on the table and stood up.

'If you'll excuse me,' he murmured and quickly left the room.

Mr and Mrs Thornycroft exchanged dark looks across their plates.

'That boy will lead me to an early grave,' Mrs Thornycroft said between clenched teeth to Mrs Bailey. 'He is totally uncontrollable!'

There was an awkward pause while everyone shifted in their chairs.

'And how is your lovely house?' Scotchie's mother continued, fixing the smile back on her face. 'Have you decided on the carpet yet?'

Immediately after the dishes were cleared, I went to find Scotchie. He was stretched out on his bed, his shoes still on.

'Bit rude, wasn't I? I'll never hear the end of it,' he groaned.

'Actually, I think you did very well, all things considered.'

'Shit! They're such reactionary pigs!' Scotchie shouted and raced out the door.

From the balcony I watched him running wildly through the bush, dodging trees as he raced towards the river. He disturbed a flock of white cockatoos, which flew up into the sky, screeching loudly. Scotchie stopped in his tracks to gaze up at them, before he turned and began walking slowly back towards the house. Noticing me on the balcony, he waved and then, suddenly and unexpectedly, he did a handstand. I laughed and ran down the steps to join him.

SIXTEEN

In November a hush seemed to fall over Melbourne while the HSC exams were on. Mrs Thornycroft drove Scotchie in for each exam and home again afterwards. Perhaps she wanted to make sure that her wayward son did in fact attend.

The day after Scotchie's final exam, Mr and Mrs Thornycroft left for England, taking Fiona with them. To celebrate his twofold freedom, Scotchie immediately headed towards his beach house with a couple of mates.

Meanwhile I enrolled in the local high school for the following year, having convinced my parents it was absolutely necessary for me to change schools. It had been a monumental battle, but the fact that my father had gone to a high school and had still managed to become a doctor, helped me to victory. On the last day of the term I walked out the elaborate wrought-iron gates of my exclusive private girls school, overjoyed that I was leaving it all behind me. Besides, it was the summer holidays.

The minute I arrived at Shoreham, I set off to see Scotchie. Parked in the driveway was a shiny new white panel van, while inside the house, two complete strangers were sitting in the living room.

'Hello,' I said. 'Where's Scotchie?'

'He's gone up to the shop so he won't be long. You must be Lucy,' replied a dark-haired boy. 'I'm Spike.'

I noticed that he was rather good looking.

'Have a seat,' muttered the other guy, taking his legs off the couch to make room for me. 'My name's Omo.'

'Omo? Why Omo?'

'Something to do with the way I look, or so I'm told.'

'Ah, yes.'

His face did have a sort of freshly scrubbed quality about it. Even his blond hair shone. I smiled.

'And Spike? How did you get that name?'

There was a short pause before Omo answered for his friend.

'That's his real name. With a name like that, he didn't need another one!'

Spike threw a newspaper at him but instead hit Scotchie as he walked in through the door. When my boyfriend caught sight of me, a grin spread over his entire face and his blue eyes lit up. Yet he looked different.

'You haven't had a haircut, have you?' I asked in amazement.

'Sure have,' he groaned and pretended to crawl under the couch.

'The teachers at school made him,' Omo explained. 'They wouldn't let him sit for the exams unless he cut off all his flowing locks.'

'Either the exams or my hair had to go. So what could I do? I had to give in.' Scotchie sighed bitterly before continuing. 'A wise old Chinese taxi driver once told me an ancient proverb that had been in his family for generations.'

'Which was?' Omo interrupted impatiently.

'It went something like this: "Don't let the bastards grind you down!" Then the driver tried to double the fare! Anyway, who's going to make the coffee?'

'Not me,' I said firmly.

Spike grumbled but got to his feet and collected the dirty mugs that were lying around. We all trailed after him into the kitchen. On the wall there was a mood barometer, a wooden dial with a pointer on it, which could be turned to whatever mood you were in at the time. Scotchie swung it to 'very loving' and walked towards me with his arms outstretched. However, Omo and Spike made throwing-up noises and so he wrestled me to the floor instead.

We sat around drinking coffee and listening to Bob Dylan records before Scotchie suggested going back to my place. It was very dark as we all walked up the road, especially between the streetlights.

A shadowy figure approached from the opposite direction.

'Hey, is that you, Little John?' Scotchie called out.

'Scotchie!'

When we reached him, the pair punched each other cheerfully.

'Where are you off to?'

'We're going to see Lucy's old man. Come along.'

The minute Scotchie was inside our front door he called out his usual greeting, 'G'day, Doc! How'd you be?'

'Hello, Scott. And who are these two?'

'Omo and Spike. Thought you might like some new people to argue with.' Scotchie grinned as they all took their seats around the table.

I decided to wash the dishes. My father and Scotchie always got along better if I wasn't hanging around.

'I hope you've recovered from your loss in the grand final? Bloody Hawthorn!'

'St Kilda just wasn't good enough. When you get to my age, you learn to accept these things.'

'Pity that Collingwood got bumped out in the first semi,' said Omo.

'C'arn the Pies! Hey, Little John, come over here and grab a chair,' Scotchie said as John finally arrived.

'How did the exams go?' my father asked.

They talked about when the results were due and the boys' chances of passing, before the conversation switched to politics. Scotchie and my father had differing views as to why Billy McMahon was such a terrible Prime Minister and so spent the next half hour happily disagreeing, with Omo managing to throw in a comment every now and then. Spike, obviously not able to get a word in anywhere, kept quiet while John as usual said nothing.

Omo and Spike stayed for the whole of that summer, which meant that the sitting room at Scotchie's house was completely crammed with discarded shoes, coffee cups and empty food packets. Andy, Richard and John used the place as if it were their home as well, adding their share to the domestic chaos.

The days flashed past, blurring into weeks. What warm sunny afternoons there were, we spent lazing around on the beach. But our favourite period of the day was undoubtedly night time.

I don't know how many Japanese fake-monster movies or tenth-grade Westerns we watched on television that summer but it was a lot. Hal Todd often was the host and his commercials could be counted on for a laugh as he regularly swore on camera and tripped over the microphone cord. 'Unbreakable' watches were flung against the studio wall and the seller had to race frantically around picking up the pieces.

No one ever left the room until at least the late late movie was over. Scotchie and I usually managed to get into bed then, when Andy had gone home. My sleeping arrangements seemed to amuse Omo, who never failed to recite his little joke – 'Good girls should be in bed by seven so that they can be home by ten.'

Well, I never made it home by ten; actually it was six a.m., that was the deadline. For my mother had insisted right from the start of the holidays that I had to be back by the time my family woke up. This rule, of course, was made to protect my father's innocence as he continued to be totally unaware that Scotchie and I were having sex, a fact that I would have thought was plainly obvious to any idiot. Even Andy had guessed and had come to accept it. Yet if my father chose to be blind, then it wasn't up to me to force him to face up to the truth, I decided, and so I made sure that I was home on time. After all, it was a small price to pay for my freedom.

Although Omo had some fun at my expense, he nevertheless was kind enough to allow Scotchie and me to make our little love nest in his brand new panel van. As it was parked way out the back on the lawn, it was wonderfully private, not to mention very cosy. But every morning at around five-thirty, I'd have to drag myself out of my boyfriend's arms and, with my eyes scarcely open, wander back to my own house. The sheets always felt so cold and empty when I first got into bed.

SEVENTEEN

Those few hours before I had to leave were very precious; it was the only time each day that I had Scotchie all to myself. Cuddled up together in the panel van we made love, a lot, and talked.

Once Scotchie told me about a novel that he had been writing secretly, and with the aid of a torch, he read the opening chapter aloud to me. It was about an alcoholic guy who meets a ten-year-old orphan boy on a park bench. With nowhere else to go, they share a meal of fish and chips as they discuss the past.

I thought it was a great start and told him so.

'You really think it's good?' Scotchie asked, obviously pleased with my praise.

'It's terrific! Really different from most other books that I've read. Your book is about a bum on the street, someone who actually exists in the real world and not just some phoney character that a writer has made up.'

'Even an old dero has a story to tell, and I reckon it's about time someone bothered to point that out!'

'So do you think you'll finish it?'

'Of course.'

Scotchie climbed over to the front seat and got out the passenger door. He then raised the back window of the panel van and dropped the tailgate, before leaping back into bed.

'It's bloody cold out there!' he said as he flung the torch and his papers over into the front.

We lay in each other's arms for a while without talking. Outside the sky was pink with the first flush of sunrise and a magpie began its song in the tree nearby. It was almost time to go home.

'You know, I really love the sound of the bush at daybreak. All those birds and insects. Hear them?'

'Mmm,' I murmured, listening with my eyes closed. 'I'd like to live in the country – permanently I mean, not just during the holidays.'

'Me too. My mother's place is okay but I'd like my own house somewhere. A property with hundreds of acres, stretching all the way to the mountains and back again. There wouldn't be a neighbour for miles and miles.'

Lying there quietly I could almost see the huge expanse of land.

'Every day,' Scotchie continued, 'I'd get out of bed and walk through the knee-high grass to find my favourite tree. Then I'd stand under it, fling back my head and shout "I'm awake!" for the entire world to hear.'

He would have his hands on his hips, I thought.

'And there'd be nobody to tell me to keep my voice down!'

I knew just how he felt. I had the same desperate need for space around myself as he did. Only when I was alone did I feel really free. In my imagination I pictured Scotchie in the midst of his solitary paddock and wondered if he saw me in mine. Did he realise that we shared the same dream?

He must have noticed my smile for he whispered softly, 'Lucy, I'll build you a house, one that is so beautiful you'll never want to leave. Not ever. And we can be alone together.'

I sat up and looked at him, his face now clear in the early morning light. His shining eyes, rich with promise, looked straight into mine. I loved him so much that it almost hurt. The intensity hung between us, connecting us like never before.

'So . . . what do you reckon?' he asked, waiting.

'Okay,' I finally managed to say, beginning to breathe again.

EIGHTEEN

Finally the HSC results came out. Scotchie, I'm very glad to say, had passed. He raced about the room like a maniac, hugging everyone in sight. His marks even made it possible to get into Arts at Melbourne Uni, which had been his (and his mother's) first choice. Omo and Spike had also made it. John was headed for Social Work at La Trobe Uni. So the celebrations continued far into the night and there was not much left of my father's alcohol stores by the next morning. However, it was my father who generously kept insisting that they open bottle after bottle.

'To success!' he shouted, waving his glass in the air for yet another toast. 'Good on you, boys!'

Despite Scotchie's raging hangover the following afternoon, he managed to make it to the post office in order to send a telegram to his mother, who was still in London.

That same day we received news of another kind. Mr and Mrs Bailey, the couple I had met in Eltham, rang to say that they would be arriving in two days' time. Mrs Thornycroft had given them free use of the beach house during her absence and they had decided to take her up on the offer.

Scotchie was furious as he put down the phone and yet helpless in the face of his mother's promise. We began an extensive clean-up operation, grumbling all the while. Omo and Spike moved their things into a side bedroom, but Scotchie refused to be anywhere near 'those fascist bastards' and frankly I didn't blame him.

So we shifted the sitting room into the garage. This involved carting out all the rusty old tools to make room for the big couch, some chairs and the television. With this new arrangement, the Baileys didn't disturb us much. Once they asked us to shut the garage doors, but after we put John in charge of the television's volume control, we managed to keep the noise level down and settled into peaceful coexistence.

Mind you, it was rather cramped in the garage. Somehow Omo always wangled his way into the prime spot on the couch, while Scotchie and I generally scored a place beside him. John was given his own special chair, a solid wooden one. Spike, Richard and Andy sat wherever they could.

Another boy in the area also began to hang around Scotchie's place and had to be accommodated. Although Greg was only thirteen, he could play many of Bob Dylan's old songs on his guitar, much to Scotchie's delight, and even knew the chords to John Lennon's new song 'Imagine'. Naturally we would all sing along.

One evening we discovered another of Greg's assets: his mother. She came over to give him a phone message and politely knocked on the broken garage door.

'Hello. Is Greg there?'

'What do you want?' her son answered, emerging from the gloom.

She gave him his message and began to leave, but Scotchie called out, 'Hey, don't go yet. Pull up a pew and someone will get you a cup of coffee, won't you, Spike?'

I leaned across and gave Richard a push. He graciously gave up his seat for her before swiping Spike's empty chair.

'Well, I might just stay for a little while. We don't have TV at our house. What are you watching?'

'A whole lot of crap is on at the moment, but an Errol Flynn movie is starting soon. Greg can maybe give us a song till then,' Scotchie suggested.

Greg shook his head and frowned pointedly at his mother. She refused to take the hint and introduced herself as Pat.

'Goodness, the mosquitoes are bad here, aren't they? Why are you all in the garage? Surely the house would be more comfortable.'

Spike handed her a cup of coffee and I passed the Aerogard over.

'My mum's overseas and she lent the house to a few of her buddies,' Scotchie explained with a trace of bitterness in his voice.

'That's a bit rough if she knew that you're already here,' Pat said and was rewarded with a smile.

'Look, it's your commercial, Omo!' interrupted Richard and began to peg out imaginary clothes along a washing line.

'Just feel how clean his skin is,' Andy laughed, swivelling around to pinch Omo's smooth cheek.

'So, Pat, what do you do for a living? Or do you live off your old man's money?' Scotchie asked.

'As a matter of fact, I'm a teacher.'

'Yeah?'

The rest of us echoed his horror.

'An English teacher,' Pat added.

'Scotchie got ninety-one for English Literature in his HSC results,' Andy informed her proudly.

Scotchie grinned and swung his feet happily.

'You certainly didn't get ninety-one for personal hygiene, that's for sure,' Omo broke in, his hand over his nose. 'When was the last time you changed your socks?'

There had been a lot of complaints recently about the way Scotchie's socks smelt but nothing was ever done about it. As always, he ignored the remark and turned towards Pat.

'Have you read any Wilfred Owen?'

'He happens to be one of my favourite poets!' she laughed.

So naturally Pat became an instant mate of Scotchie's and the pair settled down to a long discussion about several particular poems. Eventually it was interrupted by John's order for silence. The movie had started.

After that night in the garage, Scotchie often went over to Pat's house in the afternoon. He appeared to forgive her for being a teacher and she, in turn, must have overlooked his rough edges. It did seem funny, though, how well Scotchie got on with other people's parents when he had such difficulty with his own.

Yet when I thought about it some more, I realised that Andy and Greg didn't share Scotchie's enthusiasm for their respective parents. It must be easier to get along with an adult when there's no blood tie to mess things up, I finally concluded.

When Scotchie went off to visit Pat, I took Spike horseriding. Because Gina was at some political summer school in Sydney, her horse was growing fat in the paddock and so it was terrific to have someone to exercise him. Besides, I was glad of the company. Although we didn't talk much, I liked the way Spike always bought both horses an icy-pole if we passed the shop.

We were all frequent customers at that general store. Omo, in particular, needed a constant supply of food to fill his stomach while Andy's chief source of amusement was to annoy the poor shopkeepers. He would slouch in, imitating the way Scotchie walked, and shout, 'Musk sticks all round!' Then he'd slap a borrowed ten-dollar note down on the counter and wait impatiently for the change. At least one expedition up to the shop was necessary each day.

'Phew! I didn't realise it was so warm today,' Scotchie said, taking off his denim jacket as we began to walk there, one morning in late January.

'Can you imagine what it's going to be like going back to school next week in this kind of heat?' moaned Andy.

'Just think of me at the beach, kiddo. Being a uni student, I've got a whole extra month of holidays.' Scotchie proudly slung his jacket over one shoulder before yelling out, 'Hey, Omo, isn't that right?'

But Omo was concentrating too hard to hear. It was his habit to walk slightly in front, his eyes firmly fixed on the ground as he searched the roadside for money. It did seem to be worth his while, as he often netted several dollar notes – not that he ever shared his good fortune with us. Nor did he actually need the money. His father was loaded, and had given him the brand new panel van for his eighteenth birthday.

Suddenly we heard a car coming and Scotchie put out his thumb. It was the Baileys, who pretended not to see us.

'What are you doing?' called John from further down the hill. As usual he was a long way behind.

'Hitching, of course.'

'It's not even a quarter of a mile to the shop.'

'Yeah, but it's a bloody steep hill. Anyway, why walk when you can ride?'

'Then why didn't we bring the panel van?' came John's sensible reply.

''Cos it's more fun like this.' Scotchie laughed.

John shook his head. 'Sometimes I think that you're absolutely crazy.'

'So what?' scoffed Scotchie, and placed his jacket across his chest. Omo tied the empty arms behind Scotchie's back, straightjacket style.

'"Most people I know,"' the lunatic began to sing at the top of his voice, '"think that I'm crazy."' As he sang the Billy Thorpe and the Aztecs song, he danced all over the road.

Of course no one stopped to give us a lift, even though Scotchie managed to keep his thumb out during the entire performance. I guess that the drivers, that afternoon, must have agreed with John and decided to let the crazy hitchhiker walk.

As for John, he didn't make it up to the shop that day. When we rejoined him on the trip back, he was still muttering and shaking his head over Scotchie's behaviour. Being so busy with his thoughts, he'd walked even more slowly than usual. None of us had believed it was possible.

NINETEEN

'**B**ut three and a half weeks isn't really such a long time. We'll survive,' I said, trying to convince myself more than console Scotchie.

'It'll seem like forever,' he muttered and kicked a lump of seaweed out of his way.

My family and I were going back to Melbourne while he was staying on at his beach house with Omo and Spike.

'Before we know it, uni will start and you'll have to be back in town.'

But that made Scotchie groan even louder.

'It'll all be different then. It just won't be the same,' he wailed.

'Don't be silly! Nothing will change.' To reassure him, I curled my fingers through his in our special way.

We kissed slowly and then, holding each other close, we made our way up the track towards home.

I began at my new school and to tell you the truth, that first day I thought I had made a terrible mistake. I didn't know where my classrooms were and for a lot of the time I wandered around lost, which was incredibly embarrassing. Having boys in the class seemed strange and my uniform looked somehow different from everyone else's. Not one person spoke to me the whole day and I felt as if I was back at my old school in the role of social outcast.

Luckily, by the second week, I had met Maria. She was even shorter than me and so naturally I instantly liked her. I was soon accepted into her group, which included several Greek guys and even another half-Italian girl like me. It was great to sit in the portable classroom during lunchtimes with a whole bunch of new, exciting friends and talk about interesting things.

At the end of each day, when the last bell sounded, I'd pull my bike out of the huge stand and cheerfully ride home at top speed to ring Scotchie. Fridays were the exception, for then I would rush to catch the two trains and a bus to be with him at Shoreham.

Those weekends in February were the best of the whole summer because I actually got to sleep with Scotchie. No longer compelled to separate at dawn, we often didn't emerge from the panel van until midday. Sometimes Spike brought coffee and vegemite toast out to us, considerately disappearing again straight after the delivery. I loved having my boyfriend all to myself and not having to share him with others.

However, sadly, March brought those wonderful times in the panel van to a close. The university year began and so Scotchie moved into one of the colleges next to Melbourne Uni. It wasn't long before his phone calls were full of complaints. His room was too small and the noise of the traffic kept him awake at night. Although there was a huge park nearby, he missed the bushland of Eltham. He said that all his professors were idiots, the other students were boring and he couldn't find any of the lecture theatres. Clearly he was taking longer than I had to settle in, which made me wonder if starting university was a bigger step than changing schools.

To cheer Scotchie up, I suggested going on a date. It seemed a little weird to organise dinner in a classy restaurant and to put on a nice dress one Saturday night but I was hoping that the novelty would lift his spirits.

'Do you realise that we've never properly gone out before?' I said as we walked up Lygon Street together. 'This is our very first genuine romantic date!'

'Does this mean that I might get lucky tonight? Or will I need to wait till the second date?'

I winked at him and we both laughed.

When we entered the restaurant, a man in a black suit stopped us at the door. He glared down at Scotchie's thongs and said sharply, 'Excuse me, sir. We don't allow that kind of casual footwear in here.'

'But I bought them in Georges only last week,' Scotchie replied, grinning.

However, the man was not amused. 'Perhaps you could try the restaurant a few doors down. I believe that they're very tolerant in regard to dress standards.'

I waited for the usual smart rejoinder from Scotchie. Instead I saw, to my absolute amazement, that he was edging awkwardly out the door. Back on the street he sighed heavily.

'You know, sometimes I feel like I'm going the wrong way from everyone else. "Swimming against the tide" – isn't that what it's called?' His voice sounded strangely flat.

Nevertheless we found another place without further trouble and were soon seated at a table.

'So how's school going, Lucy?'

'Terrific! I got the top mark for an English Lit essay I did on *The Crucible* and I'm really enjoying my French classes.'

'Do you realise that if my brother Rob . . .'

'What?' I asked, puzzled about the jump in the conversation.

'If Rob hadn't transferred to the uni in Canberra,' he continued, 'he would've been living in the same crummy college as me. Imagine that!'

'That would've been dreadful. Have you—'

'I'm glad though that Omo and Spike are at uni with me.'

'I guess that you don't get to see the inside of the library much with that pair around,' I smiled.

'Dunno where it even is!' scoffed Scotchie. 'We've found the local pub and that's where the action is, Lucy. Last Thursday Omo got so drunk that—'

'You seem to be doing a lot of drinking these days,' I interrupted.

'So? Nothing much else to do.'

'What about going to classes?'

'Attendance is only compulsory at school,' Scotchie explained in a very patronising voice.

He leant back on his chair before resuming his story, 'Anyway, last Thursday at the pub, Omo left me and Spike at the bar to go to the toilet. When he didn't return, we went looking for him. He'd passed out cold sitting on the dunny! It took us half an hour to open the bloody door so that we could get him out!'

I managed a small chuckle but really I didn't find the escapade particularly funny. For me the evening was not turning out as I'd hoped.

'You know, I fainted once when I was ten. It was peak hour and I was—' I began, but Scotchie rudely waved the menu in front of my face.

'I don't want to sit here yapping all night. Let's order.'

When he's speaking, it's considered 'talking' but if it's me then it's 'yapping', I thought. I quickly reminded myself that he was having a bit of a rough time and managed to swallow my annoyance. We ordered, ate our dinners while Scotchie did a further monologue about his other misadventures before eventually we walked back to his place.

His room was in a familiar state of chaos. I sat down at his desk while Scotchie threw himself onto the bed and rolled his denim jacket into an extra pillow. After a while he muttered, 'Lucy, I don't reckon I like uni much.'

'Why not?' I asked, glad that at last we were getting to the heart of the problem.

'It's even worse than school. At school you're just a name, pushing your way up through the system. But here, you're not even that. You're given a number, a number for their files. It doesn't really matter if you show up every day or you don't, nobody cares in the slightest. You're just a big fat nothing.' Scotchie stared miserably up at the ceiling.

'A mate once gave me some good advice – "don't let the bastards grind ya down". He believed it at the time,' I reminded him.

Scotchie looked at me for a minute, deep in thought. Then suddenly his face lit up in a grin and he tenderly threw a thong in my direction.

'Yeah but that was before he realised just how many bastards he was up against! Still, I'll make them sit up and notice me. Do you see all those papers on the floor? I'm still working on that story about the old alcoholic guy. Remember? It's destined to be the world's greatest novel!'

'Oh?'

'Okay, maybe it'll be the worst,' he added, with a grimace.

I wondered to myself why it had to be one of those two extremes. Scotchie never seemed happy to settle for anything average, let alone ordinary.

So it was with some surprise that I learnt that he had joined one of the standard college clubs – the football team. Sometimes I went to watch him play on Saturdays and met up with Spike's new girlfriend. Janet was pretty, with long blond hair, and was a definite football fan.

'Look, Lucy, there goes Spike . . . wow, what a fantastic mark!'

'Mmm.' Knowing nothing about football and not wanting to learn, I went back to reading my book.

After the match was over, the boys raced across the ground to find us.

'Did you see me tackle that huge guy?' Scotchie asked, slinging an arm around me.

'No, I missed it. Sorry.'

'It was a real beauty. Phew! I could do with a drink. Let's pick up Omo and drag him down to the pub,' Scotchie suggested.

'Good idea,' agreed Spike.

'Do we have to?' I countered, without thinking.

'What? Don't you like my mate?'

'I was talking about the pub, not Omo. Can't we do something else for a change?' We always ended up at the pub, and frankly, I was sick of it.

'But Lucy, we went to that restaurant just the other night,' reasoned Scotchie.

'It was two weeks ago. Actually I was thinking of a movie. We never get to see a movie,' I said, desperately trying to alter the usual pattern of events.

'Nah. I reckon the pub.'

'And I don't,' I said firmly.

Scotchie and I stood staring at each other while the other two remained silent. They obviously wanted no part in the argument.

'Dunno about the rest of you, but I'm going to the pub,' Scotchie finally said with a shrug.

He walked off. Janet and Spike followed, leaving me to stand there alone. I watched my boyfriend kick imaginary goals as he made his way past the goal posts. Suddenly he stopped and turned to wave to me.

'C'mon, we're waiting for you,' he shouted, his voice crossing the grassy gulf that lay between us.

As we were entering the usual pub, I tugged on his arm. 'Scotchie?'

'Yeah?'

'Oh . . . never mind.'

We went inside.

TWENTY

'Will you tell me something, Helen?' I asked my old neighbourhood friend one Sunday morning. 'Do I look pretty when I'm angry?'

'Absolutely not!'

'Really?'

'Do you remember that time at my cousin's wedding and those creeps hassled us? When you told them off, your eyes narrowed into little slits and your whole face turned a disgusting shade of red. Actually, I felt like leaving with the creeps!' She laughed at the memory.

'Then why did Scotchie say that to me when we were arguing?'

'Oh, that's the oldest trick in the book. It's designed to distract you, to make you forget what you were going to say.'

'That'd be right,' I nodded bitterly. 'What's more, it bloody well worked.'

Helen gave me a sympathetic look. 'So it's not going too well at the moment?'

'No, and I don't know what I can do about it. I've tried to talk to Scotchie about our problems . . . but somehow I just can't seem to get through.' I paused, struggling hard not to cry. Helen waited patiently.

'He doesn't listen to me any more,' I said eventually. 'He's so caught up with what he's doing that he hardly ever hears a word I say. Being at uni has really changed him. It's as if he's living in a different world now and I'm not part of it. And I'm not even sure that I want to be part of it!'

'There's always the possibility that you've altered too,' my friend suggested.

I thought for a minute.

'Maybe being at a new school has made a difference to me,' I answered slowly. 'Whatever it is, it's obvious that Scotchie and I don't get along together so well any more.'

'Of course, it might just be a passing stage that you're both going through. If you give it time, it might all work out fine.'

'Perhaps,' I muttered doubtfully.

Helen hadn't given me any answers but her concern had helped. I shifted the conversation onto our HSC subjects.

I deliberately stayed away from Scotchie for several weeks, giving him some excuse about having too much work to do. I needed time on my own to sort out the confused mess in my head.

Finally we organised a weekend at my place in Prahran when my parents and Andy were at Shoreham. I thought that being alone together and away from the college might help us. I gave him strict instructions not to bring along Omo or Spike.

'G'day, mate!' he called as he came in the door. He gave me an affectionate hug.

We sat down at the kitchen table.

'Hey, I like your hat,' I said, admiring his black beret.

'Yeah, Fiona brought it back for me from Paris or somewhere. Pretty good, eh?'

'It's great! So your mother is back, is she?'

'Got back ages ago. I must've forgotten to tell you.'

He forgets to tell me a lot of things these days, I thought to myself as I watched him take off his shoes.

'By the way, I was dropped from the footy team last week. The coach reckoned I'm more trouble than I'm worth. Anyway,' he went on, 'I might try and buy a car soon. One that I can drive around the streets. Maybe I'll even get my licence! And Omo's been chucked out of his college for being drunk and disorderly or something. Ha! What do they think the rest of us are – angels?'

Then he launched into a long account about Omo's new share house and its various occupants. As usual, he made no mention of his university course.

'So what's your news?' Scotchie asked after a while.

'It's not very long until the first exams and—'

'Is this wallpaper new?' he butted in, looking around the kitchen.

'No, it isn't. Scotchie, please listen to what I'm saying.'

'Sorry,' he mumbled and chose an apple out of the fruit bowl.

As I talked about the approaching exams, he searched the apple for bad bits. Midway through, he shook his head.

'What's wrong?' I asked.

'Don't take these tests too seriously, Lucy. They're part of the stuffed-up system, you know. They only serve to put a tick or cross against people's names.'

'I happen to be one of those people,' I replied, trying to keep the edge out of my voice.

'Just don't get sucked too far into the whole HSC crap.' Scotchie took another noisy bite of the apple.

'But it's important that I pass so that I can get into uni.'

'Take it from me, uni is no great place!'

'And may I remind you about last year and how you agonised over your HSC results?' I snapped, feeling my temper rise at his unfairness.

'I was young and stupid then.'

'I need to do well. I've decided to become a teacher.'

'What? A teacher? You really have been brainwashed lately, haven't you!'

'Bloody hell!' I exploded, unable to contain myself any longer. 'I listen to one boring drinking story after another and I don't dare criticise. But when I'm talking about something that's important to me, you don't even try to understand.' I slammed my fist down hard on the table.

'Boring? Is that what you call them?' he shouted, at last putting down the wretched apple.

'Yes!'

We glared furiously at each other.

'You've done it again!' I stormed.

'What?'

'You didn't listen to the rest of what I said. We just can't seem to communicate any more. I'm about ready to give up.'

'So you want to get rid of me, do you? Okay, who's the fella?' Scotchie jumped up and savagely spun the apple core across the room, missing the open rubbish bin.

'Don't be ridiculous! Can't you see that it's not working?'

'You want out, is that it?'

'What else is there to do?'

'Right, I'll go then! You've always been a bitch anyway! I should've known better than to get involved with you in the first place!' he yelled and kicked the chair.

'Get out!'

His eyes were cold and hard as he glared furiously at me. He jammed his feet back into his shoes and left. The door thudded heavily behind him.

All was silent in the kitchen. I looked wildly around the empty room.

'He's gone,' I said aloud, 'Hurray!' and scowled fiercely at the apple core on the floor.

But Scotchie had also left a late autumn leaf, obviously picked from someone's vine as a present for me. It lay forgotten on the kitchen table. I picked it up and stared blindly at its rich colours. Scotchie never gave me flowers, I thought, only leaves. I smiled.

'He really has left,' I whispered to myself, listening for approaching footsteps.

I waited for his return for ages before, finally, I slowly moved out of my chair.

TWENTY-ONE

Two weeks later Scotchie rang.

'Lucy? It's me.'

'How are you?'

'Terrible . . . and you?'

'The same.'

'I miss you, mate.'

'Me too.'

There was a short pause. I sank into a nearby chair and forced back the tears. I fondled the telephone cord. 'I've been crying for weeks.' I said.

'Yeah.'

Another silence as we both remained locked inside our wordless misery.

'John and I are going up to Canberra this weekend to see Rob.'

'Oh.'

'Do you wanna come?'

'I don't think that's such a good idea.'

'I reckon it is.'

'Okay.'

I heard the relief in his voice echo down the line.

'We'll pick you up at your place. Four-thirty, Friday.'

'Right. Bye.'

'See you.'

My father came into the room and caught me still clutching the telephone receiver. I put it down hurriedly.

'Was that Scott?' he asked.

'Yes.'

'You didn't talk for long.'

As I said nothing, he continued, 'He hasn't been ringing much these days.' My father searched my face for clues.

'I guess not,' I answered and escaped to my room.

Half an hour later it was my mother's turn. She knocked gently on the door.

'Dear, can I come in?'

'What do you want?'

'Lucy, what's the matter? Is it Scott? Why don't you let us try to help?'

'It's none of your damn business!' I snapped.

'Look here, you've been behaving like this for weeks,' my mother retorted. 'It's obvious that there's something wrong but there's really no need to take it out on me.'

'Why can't you just leave me alone?'

'Because I'm worried about you.'

'Sure,' I replied sarcastically, although I knew that I was being unfair. I sighed. 'Mum, I'm going to Canberra this weekend with John and Scotchie.'

'In John's car? But what sort of driver is he? It's an awfully long way to go for a weekend, isn't it?' She immediately began to fuss.

'Shit!' I yelled. 'You don't like it when I don't tell you anything but when I do – it's even worse!' I threw myself down on the bed and closed my eyes. When I looked up again, my mother had gone.

But going to Canberra was a mistake. Everything, right from the start, went wrong. Scotchie was drunk when he arrived at my place and we had to stop along the way so that he could throw up. Rob was not at all pleased to see his younger brother when we arrived and deliberately ignored him. Scotchie and I spent the whole time arguing; we just couldn't seem to agree on anything. We even argued about the places we wanted to see in Canberra. I guess that neither of us could forget the last terrible fight we'd had, no matter how hard we tried. The damage had been done; the rift between us was now all too obvious.

On Sunday afternoon we began the long journey home. John drove steadily down the Hume Highway, his huge hands gripping the steering wheel. Scotchie sat behind him on the back seat but neither of us spoke, each looking out of our separate windows. There was nothing left to say.

At last, somewhere near Seymour, I turned to Scotchie. The tension was unbearable.

'It's no good, is it?'

He didn't reply, but kept his face turned towards the window so that I couldn't see his expression.

'We've lost it,' I added. I had completely run out of hope.

Suddenly Scotchie gave a strangled scream. He threw himself against the door and frantically struggled with the door handle.

'What are you doing?' I cried.

'Got to get out. Now!' he shouted and flung the car door wide open.

I saw the tarmac flashing below and grabbed him just in time while John swerved off the road, screeching to a halt.

'What the hell do you think you're doing?' he demanded as he twisted around to slam the door shut.

'I want to walk home from here. On my own.'

'Don't you ever do that again! You could've been killed.'

Scotchie only shrugged his shoulders as John firmly locked the door.

We continued down the highway in deathly silence. Scotchie slouched in the corner, his eyes shut. I looked out the window at the vast expanse of emptiness.

We both knew it was over.

TWENTY-TWO

With the passing of the weeks, the gulf between Scotchie and me slowly widened. For me the distance was hard to bear and there were many nights when I agonised over the decision I had made. I wrote to him often – letters born out of the cold sweat of midnight loneliness – but in the clear light of morning, I would throw them away. Our relationship was over and so I missed Scotchie in silence. Even as I wrote those letters of love, I knew that they would only confuse and cause more pain if I sent them. I let him go and lived the torment of our separation in private.

One Friday evening, about a month later, my mother and I went to see a play at Melbourne University. Finding myself so close to where Scotchie lived, I decided to visit him afterwards. It took a while to convince my mother to stop off at his college on the way home, but finally she agreed when I promised to be only fifteen minutes.

I ran up the stairs, heart pounding, and knocked on his door before I entered. Scotchie was there, slumped at his desk.

'Hello, I just thought I'd drop in,' I said, strangely overwhelmed by shyness.

A pair of dull blue eyes turned to look at me.

'Oh, it's you.'

'How's it all going?'

'Shithouse.'

'What's happened?'

'Nothing.'

He swivelled back to face the wall, placed his elbows on the desk and rested his head on his hands.

'How's that great book of yours?' I tried again.

'My tutor reckons that it's crap. I threw it away.'

There was a heavy pause while I stood against the door, not knowing what to say. After a moment Scotchie spun around to glare at me.

'Just piss off, Lucy.'

'Are you okay?'

I walked across the room and gently touched him on the arm. But he jumped to his feet, his face contorted with fury. He began to wrench books out of the bookcase and smash them against the wall.

'Hey! What are you doing that for?'

'You bitch! Why are you here?' he screamed.

'To see you, of course. Because I'm stupid enough to care about you!' I shouted, edging backwards towards the door.

Our eyes locked. Scotchie stood still, letting the books fall from his hands.

'Don't go,' he said. 'I'm sorry, Lucy.'

I sat on the corner of the bed, watching him carefully. He started to pace up and down like a caged animal.

Then suddenly he threw himself face down on the carpet. His entire body was shaking. I went over to sit beside him.

'Is it because I left you?' I asked gently.

'No.'

'Well then, what's wrong?'

'Everything.'

To my horror I saw that he was crying. He jerked his head away, burying his face in an arm.

'Scotchie, tell me what the matter is,' I pleaded.

But he didn't say a word. He just cried louder, his body wracked with sobs. I stroked his back, trying desperately to calm him. Yet with every passing minute, his pain seemed to grow more intense. He threw a hand wildly up to his head and ripped out some hair.

'Stop it!' I demanded but he continued to pull out clumps of hair. Nothing seemed to matter to him, except the violence of his agony. He appeared lost inside a terrible, dark world and clearly I was unable to reach him. Finally I just sat beside him, feeling useless and frightened.

'I have to go. My mother is waiting. I'll try to come back. Okay?' I said, hoping that I'd kept the trembling out of my voice.

Scotchie made no sign at all that he'd heard me. I opened the door slowly. He didn't look up. I left him there, still lying on the floor howling. I raced back to the car.

'Mum!' I cried frantically. 'Something is really wrong with Scotchie.'

However, my mother didn't listen. Instead she shoved her watch in front of my face.

'I'm absolutely furious with you!' she shouted. 'I've been waiting here for a whole hour.'

'I'm sorry, but I have to go back.'

She shook her head emphatically. 'I should never have agreed to let you visit him in the first place. I knew it would only lead to trouble.'

'I can't leave.'

'Lucy, I've had enough of your ridiculous moods lately and I'm not going to sit in this freezing car for another second.'

'That's okay, I'll catch a taxi.'

'For goodness sake! This nonsense has got to stop. Get into the car immediately!' she ordered.

'No! I'm staying!'

'I am not leaving without you! And that's that!'

My mother threw open the passenger door and waited.

I was the one who broke; I simply couldn't take any more. I got into the car.

I watched the lights of the college disappear through a blur of tears. My mother drove along the empty streets without a word. How I hated her! But even more than that, I hated myself for giving in to her and for leaving.

'Oh Scotchie,' I wept soundlessly to myself, 'I didn't mean to go, really I didn't. But you frightened me and I didn't know what to do. Why . . . why were you crying, Scotchie?'

He never told me. Perhaps he didn't know.

He didn't mention that night in the letter I received from him one month later.

Dear Lucy

I've moved to La Trobe Uni. I'm writing this letter while looking out my window where I can see a beautiful lake with ducks circling. It's peaceful here and I think of you a lot. I know you don't love me as you did, but I hope that we'll always be special to each other. I treasure all those times we had together. Take care of yourself.

In loving friendship,

Scotchie

I read this letter over and over again. His shadow seemed to have passed. I was glad. I suppose it made me feel a little less guilty about him.

TWENTY-THREE

I was pleased that Scotchie had transferred to La Trobe University, for John was there too and could keep an eye on him and give me updates about how he was going. Scotchie apparently wasn't studying much, rarely bothering to go to his lectures. However, John reported that he seemed happy enough and had a busy social life with lots of new friends.

After a month had passed, John told me about one friend in particular. He hesitated slightly before informing me about Liz, Scotchie's new girlfriend. She was a first-year student and lived in the same college. She was pretty. I didn't listen to any more details after that.

Anyway, by August I'd met Michael. He'd just turned nineteen when he spun into my life on a motorbike, wearing a brown leather jacket and very cool sunglasses. He had long blond hair, which sometimes he allowed me to plait, and he was extremely good-looking. Smart and creative, he was doing a course in Architecture. I adored him. However, my father took one look at my new boyfriend and instantly knew that I was having sex. Luckily I had the perfect excuse for spending my weekends with Michael – one not even my father could argue against.

For Michael was helping me with my schoolwork. As my Australian History teacher had had a nervous breakdown in June and hadn't been replaced, Michael was taking me systematically through each topic on the Australian History curriculum, using his notes and essays from the previous year when he had got an A for the subject. These hours weren't exactly the highlight of our weekends together, but I guess we couldn't make love the entire time and besides, I really did need the coaching.

My fellow classmates weren't as fortunate. The situation was so unfair, I thought one day as I waited for them. It never would have happened in my old school. I remembered back to another world, of state-of-the-art new buildings with teachers who spoon-fed their pupils. Subjects were allocated whole areas, such as the science wing and the art studios, and there were specific areas for different kinds of sports, such as the hockey oval, basketball courts, and an enormous indoor gymnasium. We actually felt deprived because there was no swimming pool, as there was at other private girls schools! I looked at my current school's ugly red brick building, which housed most of its classrooms, except for those out the back in the portables. In the forecourt was the bitumen quadrangle that doubled as our one-and-only sportsground and our place of assembly. No gym, hall or special wings for this high school.

My friends arrived to find me fuming.

'It's outrageous that we don't have a teacher for HSC! How do they think we're going to get into uni without one?' I raged before they even had the chance to sit down. 'As students we have certain fundamental rights and a teacher is one of them!'

Of course Maria and the others agreed; we were all totally fed up. We decided to call a school-wide strike, which became the first of many. Not that it made any difference, not even when we marched alongside thousands of other disgruntled secondary students in September, calling for better educational facilities. We never did get an Australian History teacher.

As the exams loomed, we gave up protesting and returned to our individual desks for study marathons. Weeknights I revised my main four subjects and during the weekends Michael and I went over the key events in Australian History. I sat each exam in turn and to my immense relief, discovered no terrible surprise question on any of the papers.

Straight afterwards I managed to get a job minding two small children, in order to save up some money for a trip that Michael and I were planning. However, I negotiated a break over Christmas so that I could spend the week at Shoreham.

On Boxing Day there was an unexpected knock on our front door.

'G'day,' shouted a familiar voice and in walked Scotchie.

'Well, hello!' my father exclaimed, with a quick glance in my direction. 'I was worried that you might give our place a miss this year.'

'Not a chance!' Scotchie grinned and threw himself into a chair.

Happily I went to get the traditional bottle of beer out of the fridge.

'How did the exams go?' Gina asked after introducing her boyfriend Paul to Scotchie.

'Not so good. In fact, I failed a couple of subjects.'

'That's dreadful! What on earth happened?' said my mother, clearly shocked.

'I guess there was too much wine, women and song – not to mention the drugs!' Scotchie laughed.

'Drugs? What drugs?' My father raised his eyebrows sharply.

'What about trying to get into Dookie Agricultural College?' I suggested hastily.

'Why on earth would I want to go there?' Scotchie asked, before continuing, 'Anyway, I've decided that I'm gonna take next year off. My brain needs a bit of a rest.'

'That's a shame because Lucy will probably be at La Trobe Uni next year,' Andy piped up. 'By the way, have you got rid of Liz yet?'

'So how's your family?' asked Gina, changing the subject after a quick scowl at our brother.

'Okay, I guess. When Rob turned twenty in July, he registered for military service like the little conformist shit that he is, but he wasn't called up. Anyway, isn't it great that Whitlam put an end to conscription!'

The conversation turned to politics until eventually my parents and sister disappeared off to bed. Andy hung around for ages, quizzing Scotchie about what he'd been doing, before finally he too left the room, giving me an encouraging little wink on his way out. It had taken him months to adjust to the fact that Scotchie was my boyfriend and now he was obviously having trouble accepting the break-up.

At last Scotchie and I were alone.

'How have you been?' I asked.

'Okay, I guess. And you?'

'Fine.'

There was an uneasy pause. Suddenly Scotchie groaned miserably.

'Lucy . . . I failed. Rob is off to Harvard and I bloody well failed first year uni.'

'Listen, you changed universities part way through the year. That surely wouldn't have helped your marks,' I said.

'I suppose not,' he replied but his voice was heavy with self-doubt.

He got to his feet and wandered aimlessly around the room, picking things up and putting them down again immediately.

'Gotta go,' he suddenly announced.

Surprised, I saw him to the door and switched on the outside light. I watched him, hands in his pockets, slouch off into the night.

Two nights later he reappeared, accompanied by Greg. Already seated at our table were John and Richard, playing cards with Andy and me.

'Brilliant timing, Scotchie! We're just about to start a new game. Pull up a chair,' Andy told him.

However, Scotchie shook his head.

'How's Pat getting along?' John asked, dealing the next round.

'My mother? Oh, she's all right,' Greg answered, examining his cards before adding, 'And that reminds me, Scotchie, she loved the book you gave her for Christmas.'

'So you still visit Pat, do you?' Richard asked.

'Yeah.'

Scotchie began to fidget with a box of matches while the five of us played on.

'I reckon I'll go for a walk along the beach,' he finally announced.

'Okay, just wait till this round is over,' I said. It looked like I was going to win.

'Nah, I wanna go alone.' Scotchie marched straight out the door.

We all stared at each other, bewildered. John and I threw in our cards.

'What's up with him?' Richard demanded, but no one could think of a reply.

Andy angrily leapt to his feet. 'What did you do?' he shouted, glaring at me.

'Nothing! Scotchie obviously just wants to be on his own,' I replied.

'Why doesn't he visit us much these days?'

'It's not my fault . . . is it?' I said, looking to John for help.

'Lucy is not to blame,' he agreed. 'People sometimes change. Things can't always stay the same, even if we want them to.'

John put his coffee mug in the dishwasher and lumbered off home. Richard and Greg left soon afterwards. I decided to go to bed although it was only ten o'clock. For there was nothing else to do at that time of night, not now.

TWENTY-FOUR

According to John, Scotchie was seeing a psychiatrist. 'Come on,' I said, with a laugh. 'Scotchie's always been a bit of a lunatic!'

However, John wasn't finding it at all amusing and I wondered to myself whether his Social Work course was starting to affect him. He certainly was treating this whole business far too seriously.

'It was his mother's idea,' John explained.

'Naturally!' I sneered. I put my cup down on the table with a bang.

'You don't understand. He tried to run over Mrs Thornycroft in the driveway at Eltham. Luckily she jumped out of the way, just in time.'

'Pity!' I muttered sourly.

'Scotchie hit an embankment. The Citroen is pretty smashed up.'

I went to get some more coffee.

'Lucy, he really isn't too good,' John continued when I sat down again. 'He's living in a shed that only has three walls to it, with no electricity. It's miles out in the bush and he hardly sees anybody.'

'So what? He's always wanted to be a hermit,' I said quietly, remembering.

Ordinarily I enjoyed catching up with John in the coffee shop at La Trobe Uni where I had begun an Arts–Education course. The few friends from school who had managed to get into uni were at Monash, as was Gina. Even my mother had begun a part-time course there! My boyfriend Michael went to Melbourne. Consequently I was usually hanging around campus on my own, surrounded by a multitude of strangers, unless I was lucky enough to spot John's familiar face in the crowd.

Travelling to La Trobe from Prahran took me ages, so it wasn't long before I decided to move into Michael's shared house in Carlton, which was on a direct bus route to Bundoora. Once a week I returned to sleep in my own bed at my parents' house to keep up the pretence that I hadn't actually moved out of home. That way everyone was happy.

One night while I was sitting at Michael's desk, struggling with an essay, I decided to write a letter to Scotchie. I sent it to his mother's house, hoping that it would somehow reach him.

It was early evening, a month later, when I opened the door to a visitor.

'Scotchie!' I cried, hugging him.

I stood back to look at him. His hair was longer and even wilder than before. He shifted his weight uneasily and avoided my eyes.

'I'm sorry, come in,' I quickly added and dragged him by the hand down the long passageway.

'It's great to see you.' I smiled as we sat down at the kitchen table.

Scotchie gazed silently around the room.

'Nice place, isn't it? I've been living here for a couple of months. There are four of us, all students, and we share the cooking.'

'Oh.'

'By the way, Scotchie, you turned out to be right about uni.'

'Did I?' His eyes stared at a poster on the wall.

'No one is very friendly there, are they?'

'No.'

'And two months ago Dad had another heart attack and was in hospital for three whole weeks. I wanted to call you but you aren't on the phone.'

To my surprise Scotchie didn't appear particularly interested. I instantly realised that I'd hardly given him a chance to speak.

'So what's up with you?' I asked.

'Nothing much.'

I waited but he didn't go on.

'What have you been doing?' I tried again.

'Not a lot.' He still didn't look at me.

'Have you got your licence now?'

'Yeah.'

I stared at him. He fidgeted with the spoon in the sugar bowl.

Suddenly Scotchie stood up and mumbled, 'I have to get going now.'

'So soon?' I clutched his sleeve as he began to leave the room.

'Is there something wrong?'

He hesitated.

'Please stay,' I begged.

Scotchie slowly turned to face me. Our eyes connected for the first time.

'Can I have some toast?' he asked. Unexpectedly he grinned. 'With Vegemite?'

'Of course.'

He sat down again. After eating his toast, he became talkative.

'Have you heard about the shack? That's where I live these days, although it's really freezing. Omo came over one day and helped me rig up some plastic over the open side but the wind keeps blowing it off.'

'How about putting in a proper wall?' I suggested.

'Last week the snake of wisdom chased me around the house at Eltham,' Scotchie went on.

'What?' I blinked.

'But it decided not to bite me. I guess I wasn't ready for it.'

'What are you talking about?' I asked, laughing nervously.

Scotchie's face remained perfectly serious.

'Never mind. Forget it.'

Fear began to coil itself around the pit of my stomach.

Just then Michael arrived home. Scotchie watched my boyfriend make himself a cup of coffee and decided to leave. This time I didn't stop him.

As Scotchie was getting into his car, I said, 'Since you're not on the phone, you'll have to ring me. You will keep in touch, won't you?'

'Sure,' he answered.

But he didn't.

TWENTY-FIVE

Many months passed, without one single word from Scotchie. I wondered why he made no effort to see me and began to feel rather hurt about it all. However, I soon realised that I was not the only one being ignored. John was no longer allowed to visit the shack, although he wasn't given any particular reason.

Spring changed to summer and it seemed as if Scotchie was going out of his way to avoid everyone. At Christmas time Michael and I ran into him on the beach but he was ready with some garbled excuse and quickly escaped. Andy, too, met with the same cold shoulder. Once my father managed to catch Scotchie as he walked past our front gate. This summer there was no 'G'day Doc!' and no sitting around the barbecue. Instead Scotchie remained firmly on the other side of the fence during the five-minute conversation. Afterwards my father came inside and shrugged his shoulders in a worried kind of a way. It was clear that he hadn't got any more sense out of Scotchie than we had.

Yet not one of us had the faintest suspicion about what Scotchie was to do next. Perhaps we were all too blind to recognise the warning signals. Or maybe there were none. It was impossible to know.

It was a warm night in January and I was back at Shoreham for the weekend without Michael. John, Richard, Andy and I headed along the familiar track towards the beach, armed with two torches. Arriving on the beach, we stopped to wait for John. Andy decided to sit on top of a rubbish bin, which unfortunately came away from its post. As he was attempting to fix the damage Richard asked him, 'Have you decided on a career yet?'

I realised with a jolt that my brother was about to start HSC.

'Maybe engineering,' Andy replied, trying to hammer a screw in with his shoe.

'Good idea! Then you could invent an unbreakable rubbish bin!' I laughed.

'Engineering?' Richard sounded surprised. 'But won't your father want you to be a doctor like him?'

'Why should he? The decision is up to me.'

'What decision?' asked John as he finally arrived. 'Hey, what have you done to that bin?'

'Nothing,' Andy unexpectedly snapped. 'It was like that when we got here.' He marched off, leaving the ruined bin behind.

We all slowly wandered along the shore until we reached the rocks. Then we turned around and walked back. Nobody seemed to have much to say and eventually we sat down to watch the lights across at Phillip Island flicker on and off.

'The tide's coming in,' John said.

Andy was drawing patterns in the sand while Richard lit up a cigarette.

'I wonder when the moon is—'

'Who cares!' Andy interrupted rudely. 'Why the hell isn't he here?'

'Because he doesn't want to be,' John answered calmly.

'It's bloody boring without him!'

'Who are we talking about, by the way?' asked Richard, but his ridiculous question was ignored.

'He's turned out to be a real bastard!' Andy went on angrily. 'I mean, a fella can't just walk out on his mates like that.'

'Of course he can. He's free to do whatever he chooses.' John was always so reasonable.

'Ah, Scotchie,' Richard muttered to himself, finally realising.

'Fair enough if he doesn't want us as friends any more, but surely he could manage to say "Crappy weather we're having. Gotta rush, be seeing you" or something when we run into him,' I said, the bitterness creeping into my voice more than I intended.

'Yeah,' Andy agreed. 'Anybody would think that we'd never met the guy before, the way he treats us.'

'Why don't we find him right now and tackle him about it?' suggested Richard.

'I suppose we could ask him why he's acting this way towards us,' my brother said slowly.

'What do you think, John?' I asked.

'I doubt if it can do any harm.'

'Right!' Andy said, leaping to his feet. 'He might be at Pat's place. Let's try there first!'

It was Greg who opened the door.

'Oh hello,' he said, 'we thought you might turn up.'

Dazzled by the bright lights we followed him, blinking, down the corridor. Pat was sitting in her dressing-gown, watching television.

'So when did you get this?' Andy asked, pointing towards the screen.

Pat got up and flicked the TV off.

'You've heard the news then,' she murmured strangely, looking into our eyes, before disappearing into the kitchen to fill up the kettle.

'What's happened?' John asked, sounding nervous.

'Hey Mum, it seems that they don't know about Scotchie, after all,' Greg called into the kitchen.

'Scotchie?' I echoed, my heart beginning to pound.

Pat came back into the room and sank into a chair, the coffee forgotten.

'He's all right, Lucy. He's been taken home to Eltham this afternoon. Last night . . . he had a bit of an accident . . . well, sort of an accident. He swallowed a whole jar of Valium tablets before changing . . .'

'A jar of what?' interrupted Richard.

My stomach lurched; I started to feel sick.

'Valium – it's a type of tranquilliser.'

'So why did he take so many?' Richard persisted.

I glanced at John. By the expression on his face I knew that he too had guessed the truth. Andy was sitting perfectly still.

'He was trying to kill himself.'

Pat's words thudded heavily into every corner of the room. Suicide. Suddenly an image of Scotchie's blue twinkling eyes flashed across my vision.

'He swallowed all the tablets and then instantly changed his mind. Somehow he managed to leave the house without his mother seeing him. He came straight over to me. He . . . he was crying and kept repeating that it had all been a terrible mistake.'

Andy was staring fixedly in front of him.

'I raced him to the hospital where they pumped out his stomach. The doctor said that it's rare for anyone to die from an overdose of Valium, but they emptied his stomach just the same. On the way home in the car he curled up on the back seat, totally exhausted. That poor kid,' Pat said, her voice shaking uncontrollably, 'he looked so deathly pale when I took him inside his house.' She paused for a minute to steady herself.

Finally she went on, 'I had to explain to Mrs Thornycroft what had happened. She was very upset. She kept repeating over and over again, 'Scott, why? Why did you do it?' Scott hung his head in shame and didn't answer. I helped her put him to bed.'

Unable to speak, I got up to leave. The others did the same. Pat saw us to the door. Suddenly she touched me on the arm and I turned to face her again.

'I didn't . . . I didn't give him a Christmas present this year,' she whispered.

Tears were streaming down her cheeks as she quietly closed the door. Her guilt followed me into the night.

TWENTY-SIX

Patient's name: Scott Allen
Age: 19
First admitted into hospital: April 1974
Classification: Schizophrenic
Remarks: Three suicide attempts

I didn't read any further. Scotchie – a patient in a psychiatric hospital. And three suicide attempts? I shut the file, which had been carelessly left open, and placed it face down on the desk. That way the name on the front was hidden.

There was the sound of footsteps and the woman came bustling back up the corridor, straightening her uniform as she walked. She looked at the folder, scowled at me and smartly returned it to the filing cabinet.

'I'm sorry, no visitors permitted,' she informed me. 'The patient himself has requested it.'

I stared blankly at her, yet she had already resumed her typing.

'Excuse me, but—'

She looked up. 'No visitors,' she repeated firmly and went back to her work.

I had no choice but to leave. Scotchie didn't want to see me. In a daze I caught the two buses back home again.

In June Mr Thornycroft died suddenly from a heart attack. When I heard the news from John, I had an instant flash of Scotchie's visit to me after my father's first coronary, and resolved to return to the hospital and try once more to see him.

This time I was allowed in. I followed the nurse down a long white corridor, past many closed doors. We turned a corner and suddenly she stopped in front of room number eighty-seven and knocked. I went to push my hair back and noticed that my hands were shaking.

There was no answer. We set off again at a fast pace, climbed a flight of stairs and reached another corridor. I could hear voices now, becoming louder with each step I took. I rammed my sweating hands into my pockets.

I was taken into a huge room that was obviously a communal area. The nurse nodded to me and disappeared. There were a lot of people sitting around and I scanned the faces from the protection of the doorway until at last I found Scotchie, playing billiards in one corner of the room. I watched him, feeling waves of relief wash over me. He looked just the same. The old familiar Scotchie, leaning against a billiard cue as he concentrated on another player's shot. I hadn't known what to expect, and standing there, I almost laughed at my own fearful imaginings.

Scotchie glanced up and caught sight of me.

'Hey! It's my old girlfriend!' he explained to the others, and with a big grin on his face, walked over to greet me.

We sat down on some nearby chairs.

'I hope you don't mind me coming, but . . . I had to.'

'It's okay. Sometimes I don't mind visitors from outside,' he replied, his concentration still on the game he was missing.

'I just wanted to say how sorry I am about your stepfather.'

Scotchie's eyes swivelled around to look at me.

'How's your mother taking it?' I asked, suddenly realising that it was not the first time Mrs Thornycroft had lost a husband.

'She's coping, of course! Doesn't she always?'

I thought of Mrs Thornycroft, now a widow with her youngest son in a psychiatric institution, and wondered.

Scotchie restlessly started to rock his chair back and forth. I guessed that it was time to change the subject.

'So, how's it going here?' I asked, hoping that I sounded cheerful.

'Great! Everyone around this place is really fantastic. I'll introduce you to my best mate. Dave,' he shouted. 'Come over here for a minute.' Dave, as well as a few others, wandered over to join us. Scotchie had obviously made a lot of friends there. Even the nurses who walked past gave him a wink or a smile.

Soon he took me to see his room. Actually, it looked rather like his old room at the university college – small with a bed in one corner, a wardrobe in another and a desk submerged under a pile of papers.

'Poems!' Scotchie said proudly, gesturing towards the papers. 'I've been writing masses of poems. I reckon that I might be a genius, after all!'

I nodded. It was all so very familiar.

'For there's a thin line between being brilliant and being mad,' he explained. 'There have been heaps of great writers who've been mistaken for lunatics, especially poets. People only see that the guy isn't normal so they lock the weirdo up somewhere. That way the streets are free for all the boring Mr Averages. Do ya get it?'

Scotchie's eyes were burning with enthusiasm.

'But don't worry, Lucy! I'll show them,' he promised and gave my arm a reassuring pat.

I began to feel uneasy again.

'I'm sure you will. Wow, it's a superb view from here,' I remarked, glancing out of the window.

To my surprise, he leapt up and wrenched the curtain across.

'It's a bloody madhouse out there,' he shouted.

Confused, I said nothing. Scotchie stayed on his feet, pacing around the room.

'And how is the precious outside world?' he sneered.

'Okay, I guess.'

'I s'pose you're in second year at uni? Still being a good little girl, eh?' He threw the words over his shoulder as he stomped past.

'Actually I'm enjoying my course a lot more this year.'

'Studying hard, are you? That figures!'

I decided to ignore the nastiness in his voice. 'My first teaching round begins soon and I'm pretty scared about how that's going to go.'

'A budding teacher in the making – hand me a bucket, I think I'm going to throw up!'

Hurt, I remained silent. Scotchie stopped pacing to stare strangely at me, jerking his eyes wide open. I looked away quickly, remembering his own unfinished degree and switched the topic again, hoping to land on safer ground.

'Well now, what do you do for kicks these days? Do you get to go out much?'

Immediately Scotchie's mood changed.

'What the hell for?' he laughed, flinging his head back.

'I don't know, to see a movie maybe or . . .' I floundered. Another mistake.

'Nah. I don't like to leave this place too often. I mean, there's not much point. This is where reality is, you know. Right here.'

'Oh, I see,' I replied, but in actual fact I didn't understand at all.

'Goodness, look at the time!' I added after a pause. 'I'd better get going.'

'Righto. Thanks for coming round to see my new home.' Scotchie grinned.

Home? The word echoed around in my brain as I walked back down the stark, white corridor. Did Scotchie really consider this hospital as his home? As I opened the main door to leave the building, I realised that I was shaking again.

Stepping outside, I found Michael, my boyfriend, waiting for me.

'What . . . what are you doing here?'

'Thought you might need some company,' he replied gently and brushed the hair off my face.

I just stared at him, still wrapped up in my thoughts. Michael held my hand as we walked from the hospital. I didn't look back. As far as I was concerned, that place was definitely not Scotchie's home.

TWENTY-SEVEN

But Scotchie didn't stay in that place for much longer. He moved into a larger psychiatric hospital. He celebrated his birthday in there, refusing to see his family on the day, preferring to spend the time with his fellow patients.

Six months later I finally heard that he was better and he'd checked himself out of the institution. Immediately afterwards he took off in a car to travel around Australia. I got a postcard from Perth and even though I could hardly make out the scrawl, I happily stuck it onto the fridge door.

Yet it wasn't long before Scotchie was back, and back in hospital. I looked at the postcard with its photograph of people sunbaking happily on a beautiful beach and threw it into the rubbish bin.

Towards the end of the year he went to stay on his uncle's farm in northern New South Wales. John drove up to visit him during the uni holidays and said that Scotchie appeared to be all right. Apparently, he'd even been pleased to see his old mate Little John. I hoped desperately for the best, thinking that all the physical work he was doing outside might help. I guess that it did – for a while. Part way through 1976 he became a psychiatric patient once more.

I began to realise that the nightmare was not going to be over as easily as I'd initially expected. Two whole years had passed since Scotchie had first been admitted into hospital. I stared at the wallpaper in the kitchen of my new house and sighed. Life is similar to wallpaper, I thought, for just when the colours change and a different picture seems to emerge, the pattern returns to repeat itself all over again. Roll after roll, with exactly the same printed pattern. I started to worry when Scotchie's pattern was going to end.

When I turned twenty-one, Michael gave me a big party to celebrate the occasion. Everybody was there, with one important exception.

'I tell you,' Rob Allen complained into the telephone, temporarily home from Harvard University, 'that kid is like some kind of crazy yo-yo. Up, down, up, down.'

'So Scotchie is still in the same hospital?' I asked, wishing that I hadn't rung to find out.

'Well, last month he tried a few other hospitals but quickly moved back into the old favourite. He has no idea what he wants, or even where he wants to be. Who knows which hospital he will choose next week.'

'Is he okay though?'

Rob gave a bitter laugh. 'No, Lucy, he's not! Poor Mum is at her wits' end about him. What more can we do?'

As I had no suggestion to make, I soon ended the conversation and put down the phone.

When I told my mother that I was going to visit Scotchie, she insisted on driving me there. It seemed rather silly, given how far she had to come to pick me up and that I had my own car, but she was adamant.

So together we entered the hospital grounds and drove through a maze of small internal streets until we arrived at the right section. My mother turned off the engine.

'Take as long as you like, dear. I've got plenty to read,' she said, reaching into the back for her newspaper.

As I walked through the half-empty parking lot, I remembered another car park – the one outside Scotchie's college. I looked back over my shoulder to where my mother, this time, was waiting patiently for me. She obviously had not forgotten that night either. After all, the ugly hospital building was a sad reminder to both of us of our shame.

I went inside. I couldn't find any front office but fortunately a woman wandered past.

'Excuse me,' I called, 'I'm looking for Scott Allen?'

'Take a seat,' she said, gesturing towards an adjoining room, 'and I'll let him know you're here.'

She immediately disappeared.

There was nowhere to sit except at one of the enormous tables. This must be the dining area, I thought, staring around the deserted room.

At last the door swung open. I glanced up expectantly. But it wasn't Scotchie; instead a man in his thirties entered. Seeing me, he clattered noisily across the wooden floor and pulled out a chair next to me.

'You look lonely sitting here all by yourself,' he remarked sympathetically.

I managed a smile.

'It's not too bad a place, once you get to know it,' he went on.

'I'm sure it's not.'

'Have you been here before?'

'No, it's the first time. I've come to see Scotchie.'

'So you're a visitor?' he asked, surprised.

His surprise shocked me.

'Of course.'

'Oh,' he muttered, and quickly left the room.

He'd mistaken me for a patient! Me! I almost laughed. But then again, Scotchie was a patient. The joke instantly turned sour.

There was a muffled sound of footsteps and the door was slowly pushed open. I almost didn't recognise Scotchie. His skin was a greenish colour and his face was puffy. In fact, his whole body seemed bloated.

'Hello,' he said as he shuffled over in a pair of slippers and dropped into a chair. 'How are you?' he slurred, surveying me from under heavy eyelids.

'Fine,' I stammered and dropped my gaze.

'And your family?'

'They're okay. Gina has moved to Brisbane with her boyfriend Paul. How are things with you?'

He just grunted and slumped deeper into the chair.

'What have you being doing lately?' I continued.

'Nothing much.'

'By the way, Andy told me to say hi. He hopes you'll be down at the beach this summer.'

'No, the house has been sold.'

'Sold?' I echoed, aghast.

The garage, I thought. Gone. The whole world seemed to be falling apart.

'Nobody was using it.'

He spoke as if every word was an effort. His eyes closed for a second. Forcing them back open, he said, 'Last week I had electric shock treatment.'

'Shock treatment?'

'It didn't hurt much.'

I felt like screaming with horror. I imagined Scotchie's body jolting and jerking under the cruel wires.

'Scotchie, please tell me, why the hell are you here?' I cried.

'The doctors say that—'

'But what do you think is the problem?' I interrupted harshly. I really needed to understand.

'The diagnosis is that I'm manic-depressive.'

He was like some well-trained animal. I stared hopelessly at him.

Suddenly Scotchie sighed heavily.

'I was the one who found him, you know.'

'Found who?'

'My best mate, Dave.'

I waited for him to go on. When he didn't, I asked, 'I suppose your mother comes to see you?'

'He'd hung himself.'

'Oh shit!'

I leant over to touch his arm, aware of the inadequacy of my words. He wiped his nose across the edge of his sleeve before saying, 'My psychiatrist is a great bloke.'

'Oh?'

'It's rare to have a good one.'

'So what's he like?'

'Just before lunch.'

'What?'

'And it was pumpkin soup, Dave's favourite,' Scotchie mumbled. His head drooped to one side.

Soon afterwards he had to go. He was tired, he said, and needed to lie down for a while. I gave him a hug and left.

I walked slowly back to the car, concentrating on putting one foot in front of the other. My mother was looking out for my approach.

'How is he?' she asked gently.

'They've sold their Shoreham house,' I replied and put my seatbelt on, before adding, 'He's had shock treatment and he wears slippers now.'

'Oh, Lucy!' my mother whispered.

I could feel her eyes on my face but I didn't look up. I heard the engine start.

'And Mum?' I blurted, clutching her arm.

She switched off the ignition.

'Mum,' I said and took a deep breath, 'Scotchie really does have a mental illness.'

Somehow I hadn't believed it before. I guess that I just hadn't wanted to.

That night, after carefully locking the door, I sat on the bathroom floor and cried. The garage was lost forever and Scotchie's wild spirit had vanished. Try as I might, I simply didn't understand what had happened and why his life had gone so terribly wrong. It was an hour before I managed to stop crying.

TWENTY-EIGHT

Mental illness has no magical cure. Some people get better while others don't. Scotchie, as it happened, turned out to be one of the lucky ones. I don't know why he began to improve, just as I don't really understand why he went into the psychiatric hospitals in the first place. The older I get, the more I realise that sometimes there is no answer, no immediate reason, that can be given to explain a situation. Often, it just is.

All in all Scotchie was a psychiatric patient for three years. Three long years. During that time it seemed as if he was going to be there forever.

But in July 1977 he checked himself out of hospital and rented a flat in Brunswick. Cautiously I waited for further news. I didn't want to make a second mistake. A month passed slowly, then another . . . and another. This time it looked as though he was out for good.

I asked Andy to come with me on a visit but he wouldn't. He said that he couldn't bear it, and frankly, I didn't blame him. It's hard to forgive a hero who has fallen and Andy's disappointment ran very deep.

So I went alone. It took Scotchie ages to undo all the complicated locks that barred the door.

'Hello,' he greeted me when finally the door was opened. 'Sorry about the wait. Security, you know.' We sat down at a laminex table that was in the centre of the sitting room. The only other piece of furniture in the room was the television. No pictures hung on the walls. The thick curtains were drawn and the overhead light was on.

'Nice flat,' I said.

'It's not bad.'

'My brother organised it for us,' someone explained, coming into the room and joining us at the table.

'Omo?' I asked, hesitating.

I hadn't seen Omo for a very long time. I don't know what he had been doing during those intervening years but his freshly scrubbed appearance had been completely annihilated. His long, dank hair hung below his shoulders and his red face made his nickname seem like a cruel irony. I wondered if he was still a heavy drinker.

'Cup of tea?' Scotchie offered and got up slowly to get a third mug.

'Are you still working?' I asked.

'Yeah, it's a good job. We take long lunch breaks and don't have to do too much. Plus the foreman lets me come home early when I'm tired,' he told me as he poured the tea.

His hands were shaking so violently that half of my tea was spilt as he passed it across the table.

'Sorry, it's the medication I'm on that makes me a bit clumsy,' he apologised, embarrassed.

'Your mother would fire the lot of you if she knew how slack you boys are in the storeroom,' Omo said.

'What's Mrs Thornycroft got to do with it?'

'I work for her company.' Scotchie sagged against the back of his chair.

'I hear that you're now a high-school teacher, Lucy,' Omo said. 'How are you finding it?'

'Pretty tough. Most of my students come from the Housing Commission flats. They're incredibly disadvantaged. It seems silly to give them homework when they have no place of their own to study and half the time they haven't even been fed properly. These kids live such difficult lives. I'm trying to get a breakfast program happening.'

Neither Scotchie nor Omo seemed particularly interested.

'By the way,' I said, 'last week one of my students was beaten up at home and I had to call in some professional help. You'll never guess who turned up as the social worker!'

'Who?'

'John! I hadn't realised his office was just around the corner.'

Scotchie just nodded half-heartedly; visitors obviously were a strain for him.

'I live in Kangaroo Ground now,' I said, trying another subject. 'I'm renting an old farmhouse on about twenty acres.'

'I suppose you still live with . . . what's his name?'

'Michael? Er, no, didn't I tell you? He moved out a while ago.' It still hurt.

'Yeah?' Scotchie sounded interested at last. 'What happened?'

'Maybe Michael wanted . . . I could've been too . . .'

There had been problems of course, but nothing especially serious during all our years together. One morning he'd got up, cleaned his teeth as usual and left. Straight out the door. My door.

'Actually, I don't know,' I added sadly. 'Some things just fall apart.'

Scotchie nodded silently.

Omo collected the mugs and carried them into the kitchen. Scotchie momentarily rested his head on the table and I knew it was time for me to go. As I walked down the stairs I could hear the bolts sliding into place after me.

A month later Scotchie began to work upstairs in the office, filing and sorting papers. However, he soon discovered that the job was too demanding and happily returned to the storeroom.

Scotchie stayed out of hospital and that in itself was a massive step forward. It was enough.

TWENTY-NINE

'Lucy, do come in,' exclaimed Mrs Thornycroft as she opened the front door. 'Scott, you have a visitor.' Scotchie had recently moved back to his family's house in Eltham.

'This is a surprise,' he said as he clattered down the stairs. 'You're lucky to catch us in. We've just arrived home after church.' He was dressed in a dark suit and was wearing a tie. His shoes were freshly polished. I was so astonished that I almost laughed out loud.

'Church?'

'It's Sunday,' Scotchie explained simply.

Mrs Thornycroft put a protective arm around her son.

'Of course! How silly of me to . . . to forget what day of the week it is,' I stammered.

'I'm sorry, Lucy, but you won't be able to stay for long. As you know, lunch is at twelve,' Mrs Thornycroft said.

'We've still got time for a quick walk, haven't we?' Scotchie asked.

'I guess so,' she replied, checking her watch.

We walked down a narrow track that led through the bush.

'It's a beautiful day, isn't it?' Scotchie remarked.

'It certainly is.'

'How's Andy getting along? I haven't seen him for ages.'

'He's living with his girlfriend Jen now and is looking for a job.'

'What sort of a job does he want?'

'Engineering, naturally. That's what he studied at Monash.'

'Did he? I'm sorry. I have a very bad memory these days. I'm told that it's because of all the drugs I took when I was at uni.'

'Or maybe it's due to the shock treatment you had.'

'That has nothing whatsoever to do with it,' he said, clearly irritated.

We walked on. Overhead the clouds were scudding across the sky, casting floating shadows over the ground.

'Are you still working hard?' Scotchie asked.

'Yes, it seems to be all I do these days. I spend most evenings preparing for the next day's classes, trying to make the lessons interesting and relevant. But often the kids don't even turn up because school just isn't where they want to be. Sometimes I wonder why I ever decided to become a teacher.' I sighed. It had been a bad week, with several of my favourite kids arrested for starting a rumble between the Greeks and the Turks.

'So why did you, Lucy?' There was a sharp edge to his voice.

'Because I wanted to try and change one tiny corner of the whole unfair education system. You know, to help kids find their own path and become who they want to be, rather than simply conform to what is expected of them. To save just one kid from the kind of ostracism that you and I suffered at school because we were different.'

But Scotchie sighed impatiently.

'Haven't you realised by now that there's only one thing that is worth saving? And that is your own precious neck!' he snapped.

Stunned, I stopped dead in my tracks. Scotchie had obviously lost his social conscience somewhere along the road, even though he had played a crucial part in kick-starting mine.

I ran to catch up with him and tugged on the back of his coat.

'What about the book you were writing once? And all those Bob Dylan records you used to listen to? What about John Lennon's "Imagine"? Don't you care any more about people starving to death and being killed in senseless wars?'

'What are you talking about, Lucy?' he asked, startled by my behaviour.

'You were always such a fighter. If you didn't like something, you stood up and shouted! You cared! You didn't sit back, worrying about your own bloody neck then.'

'Perhaps I should have,' Scotchie answered sourly. He shrugged his shoulders.

'But what about "don't let the bastards grind you down" – remember? For there are lots of people who shoot black sheep like Dags just because they happen to be different and those bastards have to be stopped or else they'll crush you and . . .' I was almost crying.

'Am I meant to be following all this nonsense?' Scotchie interrupted calmly. 'Who is Dags, anyway?'

I stared at him in horror.

'Come on. It's getting late. We'd better head back,' he said, turning homewards.

They've won, I thought bitterly. The bastards have won!

We stood awkwardly at the door as I was leaving.

'It's nice of you to come, Lucy. I hope you'll drop by again sometime soon.' He smiled politely.

I looked into Scotchie's eyes as he stood there in the doorway. They were different eyes from the ones I remembered. Somehow they had completely lost their spark and were now dull and empty. They were the eyes of a stranger.

THIRTY

At the end of 1979 I went down to Shoreham with Andy and Jen for the usual family Christmas. We were waiting for Gina and Paul to arrive so that we could begin our roast dinner, when the phone rang. My mother answered it in the bedroom. After a few minutes she reappeared with a strange expression on her face.

'That was Rob Allen. I'm afraid it's bad news.' I put down my book.

'Scott died this morning.'

I shook my head violently. 'But I only talked to Scotchie last week and he was thinking about starting a new job . . .'

'Lucy, Rob said that he had a heart attack.'

'At twenty-five? That's ridiculous!' Andy cried.

'No!' I shouted. 'He doesn't want to die. Not any more.'

The door slammed and Andy was gone.

'He really is dead?' I whispered.

My mother nodded silently.

'What's happened?' asked my father, appearing from the sunroom.

I ran out of the house. Completely numb inside, I hurtled along the track through the pine forest, only stopping when I saw the sea stretching out below.

'Scotchie!' I cried. But the beach was empty.

THIRTY-ONE

I stared inside the hearse at the black box. It was covered with flowers. I tried to imagine Scotchie's body resting in it but it was impossible. Gina took me by the hand and dragged me away. We followed Andy up the steps.

The funeral was held in a chapel at the college where Scotchie had lived when he had gone to Melbourne Uni. I remembered how much he'd hated that place.

I tried to listen to the service but it wasn't about the person I knew. The minister's voice droned on and on about a misguided youth who had trouble settling down. I watched my father angrily shift position and my mother, her face pale, put an arm gently around his shoulders.

I wished that Scotchie could have been there to hear what was being said, but it was the old Scotchie that I had in mind. He would have sat with his feet slung irreverently over the chair in front.

'What sort of crap is this?' he would have shouted across the hushed stillness.

A smile spread over my face. The first in days.

Finally the service was over. On the way out I had to file past the Allen family. Mrs Thornycroft stood at the door, tears falling down her cheeks as she leant heavily on Rob's arm. I swallowed hard, shook her hand and muttered the appropriate sympathies. To my surprise, someone rushed forward to hug me. It was Fiona. She looked a bit like Scotchie now and I was glad.

After the cremation, many of us went back to Eltham. The food had been carefully laid out on long trestle tables. People talked quietly in groups, clinging to the corners of the room. Eyes were wiped and plates were passed.

I walked outside and gazed blindly out over the bush. There were footsteps and John appeared, carrying some glasses and a bottle.

'Beer?'

His huge hand gently brushed mine as he passed me a drink. He raised his glass to the trees and I followed suit. We drank our silent toast.

I turned to face him. Our eyes caught, connected in our shared pain.

'Why?' I asked.

'Why did he suicide? I wish I knew.'

'No, not just that. What went so wrong for him? I don't understand.'

'Me neither.'

At that moment Greg tapped me on the shoulder. He looked different with a beard and in neat clothes.

'Is Pat here?'

'Yes, she's inside talking to Mrs Thorneycroft,' Greg replied.

'Oh, there you are.' I turned to see Omo and Spike approaching.

'Hello, Spike. It's been ages. And how are you going?' I asked Omo.

'I'm okay, I guess.'

'Hi. We haven't met before, have we?' Greg asked as he extended his hand, unaware of the vast change in Omo's appearance.

'This is Brian,' Spike put in hurriedly for his friend.

Omo shrugged his shoulders. 'After all, it's my real name,' he said quietly.

We sat down on the grass. There was an awkward pause.

'So, Spike, what are you doing with yourself nowadays?' I asked.

'I'm a lawyer. I married Janet – do you remember her?'

'Of course I do.' I felt a strange stab of jealousy.

'That's right. Wasn't she there that day at the footy when . . .' Spike's voice trailed off.

Omo hastily lit a cigarette.

'I didn't realise that people still get married these days,' put in Greg.

'Janet's parents are very old-fashioned and didn't want us living together. And then she got pregnant, so we had little choice. Anyway, Janet would have come today but the baby has a bit of a cold.'

'Hey, aren't you guys going to eat? The food's fantastic!' Richard called, craning his neck around the corner of the house. He walked over, plate in hand, with Andy trailing after him. They sat down too.

'Where's Gina?'

'Talking to Rob in the kitchen,' my brother muttered.

'By the way, Andy is moving to Sydney for his new job with Ampol,' I announced.

'That's great,' replied John. 'Is Jen going too?'

'Yes.' My brother wrenched out a handful of grass.

There was another uneasy silence. No one knew what to say.

'Well,' Richard began, 'here we are.'

'Funerals are terrible, aren't they?' Spike said.

'They certainly are,' echoed Omo.

'It's a shame that the garage has been sold,' I threw in bravely.

'We had some great times there,' John added.

'We sure did,' sighed Andy.

'Do you still play the guitar, Greg?' I asked.

'No.'

'You used to play those old Bob Dylan songs so well,' I said and began to sing, '"The answer, my friend, is blowing in the wind. The answer is . . ."' I stopped. Omo's face was crumpling.

Unexpectedly there was a loud snort from John. I turned to stare at him. At the top of his voice he shouted, 'But why the hell didn't Scotchie ever wash his goddamn socks?' He started to laugh.

For a minute the rest of us just looked at each other. Then suddenly we were all laughing, remembering those dirty smelly socks.

I know that Scotchie would have liked that.

THIRTY-TWO

New Year's Eve again. I sit alone with my sadness, waiting for the clock to signal the start of a new decade. I remember how Scotchie's eyes used to sparkle and all the good times that we shared together. I raise my glass in a toast to him.

'Thanks, Scotchie, thanks for everything,' I whisper and then begin to cry, as if I will never stop.

www.ingramcontent.com/pod-product-compliance
Lightning Source LLC
Chambersburg PA
CBHW040537170726
48295CB00012B/505